CHRISTINE ANGOT

An Impossible Love

Translated from French by
Armine Kotin Mortimer

archipelago books

Library of Congress Cataloging-in-Publication Data available upon request.

Archipelago Books
232 3rd Street #A111
Brooklyn, NY 11215
www.archipelagobooks.org

Distributed by Penguin Random House
www.penguinrandomhouse.com

Cover art: Man Ray, *La main sur les lèvres* (The Hand on the Lips), 1928.
Gelatin Silver print (Estate print). 30 x 24 cm

This book was made possible by the New York State Council on the Arts with the
support of Governor Andrew M. Cuomo and the New York State Legislature.
Funding for this book was provided by a grant from the Carl Lesnor Family
Foundation. This work received support from the French Ministry of Foreign
Affairs and the Cultural Services of the French Embassy in the United States
through their publishing assistance program.

Archipelago Books also gratefully acknowledges the generous support of the Lannan
Foundation and the New York City Department of Cultural Affairs.

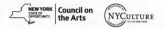

PRINTED IN THE UNITED STATES

AN IMPOSSIBLE LOVE

$\mathcal{M}$y father and mother met in Châteauroux near the Avenue de la Gare in the cafeteria she frequented, at twenty-six she had already been with the Sécurité Sociale for several years. She started working at seventeen as a secretary in a garage; he, after lengthy studies, had his first job at thirty. He was a translator at the American base in La Martinerie. Between Châteauroux and Levroux, the Americans had built a housing development on several hectares with little one-story houses surrounded by gardens without fences, in which the families of the military lived. The base had been allocated to the Americans through the Marshall Plan, at the beginning of the fifties. A few trees had been planted, but when you went by on the highway, you could see a multitude of red hip roofs scattered across a broad empty plain. Inside what was really a little village, wide paved streets allowed the inhabitants to travel in their cars, slowly, between the houses and the school, the offices, and the runway at the base. He had been hired there after his military service, he didn't intend to stay. It was temporary. His father, who was a director at Michelin, wanted to persuade him to work for the Green Guide, but he readily saw himself having a career as a researcher in linguistics or in academics. His family had lived in Paris for generations, in the seventeenth arrondissement, near Parc Monceau; they came from Normandy. In Paris, many had been doctors. They were curious about the world, they had a passion for oysters.

He invited her for coffee. And a few days afterwards for a dance. That evening she was supposed to go to a so-called "social ball" with a girlfriend. Social balls, organized by a group or an association that rented an orchestra and a large hall (distinct from the dance halls frequented by Americans and prostitutes), attracted the young people in Châteauroux. This one took place in a large exposition hall on the Déols highway, Hidien Park. My father didn't usually attend.

"Oh, I don't go to that kind of thing … We'll go out another evening. I'm going to stay home. I have work …"

She went with her friend Nicole and Nicole's cousin. The evening had already gone on for quite a long time when she saw him in the distance coming through the crowd. He approached their table. He invited her to dance, she got up, she was wearing a white skirt with a wide belt. They made their way toward the dance floor, he smiled as they arrived on the parquet floor, she was ready to slip into his arms, he took her hand to guide her and spin her around among the dancers. At that moment the orchestra began playing the first measures of "Our story is a story of love."

It was a song you heard everywhere. Dalida had inaugurated it. She would sing it with intensity, mixing the tragic with the banal. Her accent gave a roundness to the words and stretched them out at the same time, her deep voice enveloped the sounds and gave them a particular substance, there was something haunting about the whole thing. Accompanied by the orchestra, the singer imitated Dalida's original interpretation, the better to heighten the emotion.

> *Ourr storrry is a storrry of lo-o-ove*
> *Eterrrnalll and banalll it brrrings each day*
> *All the good all the bad.*

They weren't talking to each other.

> *It's the well-known storrry …*

The dance floor was crowded, it was a very popular song.

> *Those who lo-o-ove each other play together, I know*
> *My complaaaint is the plaaaint of two hearts*
> *It's a novel like so many others, which could be yourrrs*
> *It's the flame that enflames without burning*

It's the dreeeam you dreeeam without sleeping
My storrry, it's a storrry … of … a … lo-o-ove.
They were silent during the whole song.
With the hourrr when you embrace, the one when you say
farrrewell
With the evenings of anguish and the marrrvelous mornings …
And tragic or very deep, it's the only storrry in the worrrld
That will never end.
It's the storrry of a love …
They weren't looking at each other.
But naïve or very deep, it's the only storrry in the worrrld,
Our story is the storrry … of a lo-o-ove.

The song came to an end, they separated. And they went back to their table through the crowd. She introduced Nicole and her cousin to him.

They began to see each other. They went to the movies, to restaurants, to dances, they left town on the weekends, he rented a car and they left. On weekdays he met her at her office when she left work, or he went to her house. Very soon they were seeing each other every day.

She discovered a new world.

A world of intimacy, of constant talking, of questions, of answers, the slightest impression was heartfelt, personal, particular. The unexpected details, the new words. The comparisons:

surprising, radically new, contrary, daring. Ideas she had never heard expressed. Airily, he swept aside proprieties. And he described everything he saw, the places they went, the landscapes they walked through, the people they encountered, with such precision that what he said was etched inside her. He explained he had made a choice to be free, he wasn't criticizing the way others lived, but he had broken away from it. Certain things made him furious, others, which shocked her, made him laugh or moved him. God, whom she had always thought above her, did not exist for him, religion was made for the weak-minded. At the time, this was a subject that mattered.

To be left in peace, it was sufficient to make one or two concessions to society. There was the double advantage of not hurting people and of obtaining from them, when the time came, whatever they could bring you. The ideas that bothered her she put down to his unconventional personality. He would stop in the middle of a walkway, look at her, and emphasize the singularity of her intelligence; he would speak of her like a lover and an expert with the same passion as for an author he admired. As far as he was concerned, the pertinence of what she said had nothing to do with her schooling, which she hadn't finished. He made a list of educated people who were imbeciles, in spite of their high public positions. So she could profit from his experience, he explained that you have to flatter them, because to live free you have to be alone, and be the only one to know it.

Once, the radio was on, and he suddenly became angry. He criticized what he heard, hostages weeping their eyes out, asking their native countries to save them. He scorned them for valuing their personal interest above the public interest. In general, mass suffering left him cold – volcanic eruptions, earthquakes that caused thousands of human losses, it was all a matter of statistics, it didn't count as news. It was the first time she had heard that.

He would stare at her without batting an eyelash, until, overcome by her smile, the emotion forced him to close his eyes. She had a sweet smile. But never naïve. Her face was radiant but reserved. Her eyes were lively, green, sparkling, mobile – but fragile, small, worn. He talked to her about her high cheekbones, the frankness of her features, the elegance of her lips, the smile that transformed everything, and her neck, her shoulders, her belly, her legs, the softness of her skin, looking for the word that matched what he saw. He concentrated on the sensation his hands felt when he caressed her. His fingers lingered on a precise area to discover exactly what material the texture of that little zone evoked.

"Silk. It's silk, your skin."

Reading Nietzsche had turned his life upside down. After lovemaking, still lying down, he would read her a few pages. She rested her head in the hollow of his shoulder, her cheek on his chest, she listened. Then they went out, they would go to the Poinçonnet Forest, they walked along the trails holding hands. They'd met at the end of summer.

"How soft your hands are, Rachel, it's wonderful. They are not just beautiful, they're velvet. Truly like a fluid."

"Ah, do you really think so?"

"It's completely new to me. It's not just the softness of your skin, which is extraordinary. You have a potion, Rachel, I'm sure of it. Like Isolde. You too. You're making your lover drink a potion, in the hollow of your hands."

He would slip his fingers into hers like the resting wings of a little bird, sheltering in a sheath. Then: "Wait, Rachel."

He would pull them out, wiggle them in the air so they would forget the sensation of velvet they had just left. He would walk calmly beside her for several minutes with his hands in his pockets or at his sides, not touching her. Then he would put his hand back in hers, gently, slipping it again into the silky palm, which closed on it without squeezing.

"This moment when I take your hand. This precise moment, this very moment. When I slip my hand into yours. This instant. It's such a pleasure. Those few seconds. Ahhhh! It's wonderful."

He would close his eyes the better to feel, she would laugh.

"Hmmm. They're hot."

She would file her nails into an oval, polish them with an

orangey lacquer. Her fingers were long, white, her hands were large and slender, her skin was the color of weak tea, the veins visible.

Sometimes the only thing that seemed to preoccupy him was the couple they formed. He pointed out its rarity to her, and how lucky they were. He went to pick her up at her office. Leaning on the wall across the street, he smiled at her. They took Rue Victor Hugo, rounded a little nine-story high-rise that marked the center of town, dominating it, crossed Place Gambetta, and arrived at Rue Grande where he was renting a room.

"People want conjugal love, Rachel, because it brings them well-being, a certain peace. It's a predictable love since they expect it, and they expect it for precise reasons. A bit boring, like everything predictable. Passionate love, on the other hand, is linked to a sudden emergence. It disturbs order, it surprises. There is a third category. Less well known, I'll call it the inevitable encounter. It reaches an extreme intensity, and it very well might not happen. It doesn't occur in most lives. People don't seek it, it doesn't suddenly emerge either. It appears. When it's present, one is struck by its self-evidence. Its particular characteristic is that it is experienced with people whose existence one hasn't imagined or that one thought never to know. The inevitable encounter is unpredictable, incongruous, it doesn't blend with a reasonable life. But its nature is so entirely other that it does not perturb social order, since it escapes from it."

"Our encounter, it belongs to what category, for you?"

"Rachel, don't say that anymore: 'our encounter, it.' Our encounter. Belongs. To what category. The subject of the verb doesn't need to be doubled, you mentioned it, it was heard. What you are talking about was understood. I would situate it between the second and the third."

"Pierre!"

"Yes."

"… Do you love me?"

"Look at me."

"I'm looking."

"I love you, Rachel."

"I do too, you know."

They went for a walk in the public gardens, they went in from Avenue Déols, took the path along the chestnut trees that went down toward the pond, swans were gliding on the surface, there was a weeping willow, the branches hung down, rocked by the wind; they leaned on the railing and remained several minutes like that, watching in silence as the slender branches swayed and fluttered on the water, caressed it. Farther away, children were gathering chestnuts, then making them shine with a cloth. Toward the top of the park, in an immense cage, peacocks displayed their plumage. There was a bandstand. One day *La Marseillaise* resounded throughout the park. Everyone stood up from the benches, from the chairs. No one was seated. Only one guy remained conspicuously sprawled on the lawn. After a rapid glance and a shrug of her shoulders, she looked away. She continued to stand very straight.

"You're a patriot, I see, Rachel!"

"Maybe so. Maybe I am a patriot, yes. Why, shouldn't I be, you aren't?"

"I'm not shocked that this guy, who is surely exhausted from his week, is lying down on the lawn, it's Sunday after all. He came to the public gardens to relax. But I can see that you are shocked by it."

"Probably. Yes. I admit it shocks me a little."

"I'm amused by this guy. I find him quite funny."

"It's the national anthem, after all. It's a question of respect. People stand up as a sign of respect. There are people who died for us. So we can be free."

"Yesss, of course! You are right, Rachel. But do you think those who stood up here are all exemplary in their behavior?"

"Surely not, no. But I don't know if that's the question. You'd prefer us to still be occupied, do you? It's awful being occupied. We had nothing. We weren't free. In particular we had nothing to eat. There are things that can't be forgotten. I spent one whole winter in sandals. The winter of '44. There wasn't enough for my mother to cook meals."

"Where was your father?"

"My father is Jewish, as you know. He went to Egypt in '35, we were supposed to join him there. It didn't happen, it didn't happen right away, and afterwards it was too late. The borders were closed. You couldn't travel any more, nothing crossed the borders, he couldn't even send Mama money. As a Jew, it was better for him to stay there. We had no news. We had nothing. And we knew nothing. It wasn't easy. We had a neighbor, Mme Brun, she had a German lover. People in the neighborhood didn't like him, so she went to her window and shouted: 'They'll have to watch out, all these people. Mme Schwartz, wife of a Jew, and her daughter, I could hurt them.' She never actually did anything. She mustn't have been as horrible as all that, in the end."

When she met him, her mother was in a rest home in Grasse; she had a rather serious chronic respiratory illness. Her sister had just turned seventeen. They both lived on Rue de l'Indre, number 36, in a stone house with a large garden that went down to a river. You reached the river by a lane, the Chemin des Prés.

Rue de l'Indre was below Rue Grande. Number 36 corresponded to the beginning of the Chemin des Prés. The house was fifty meters down the lane. You entered a courtyard, with a metal garage at the back, beside it an unused room, the windows broken, the walls full of saltpeter. It had been her grandmother's laundry room, then her mother's ironing workroom during the war. Beyond the courtyard was the garden. The garden was separated from the lane by a little collapsed wall. The lane led to the river.

An enormous cherry tree stood in the middle of the garden. And scattered about were a peach tree, a plum tree, an apple tree. There were strawberries, flowers, iris, tulips, roses, a lilac, and, near the collapsed wall, a pear tree whose branches hung over the lane.

There was a washhouse at the end of the lane, where she did her laundry.

From the top of the stairs overlooking the garden one could see everything, down to the river. The courtyard, the garden, the water. Then your gaze was stopped by a curtain of trees. Beyond that, a shortcut led to Belle-Île, a beach on the Indre River. From this passage, you could reach the public garden through the lower gate.

Several streets defined the territory around the house. Stairs starting in Rue de l'Indre cut upward toward the center of the city. One, very narrow and dark, called la Petite Echelle, climbed after making sharp turns between the houses, between high walls, and ended behind Rue Grande at Rue des Pavillons. The other, broad and bright, called la Grande Echelle, came out behind the city hall.

The first time he came to the house, a photo had been left lying on the sideboard in the kitchen showing a group of girls, each with a paper headdress. It had been taken in the offices of the Sécurité Sociale on Saint Catherine's Day. There was a party that day. Unmarried twenty-five-year-old girls wore a headdress, a *coiffe*, they "coiffed Saint Catherine." "Catherinettes" they were called. The purpose was to show them off before they became old maids. The employees in question had constructed their hats with paper, scotch tape, and staples, and an aperitif had been served after the workday. She was in the last row with the tallest girls, head thrown back, laughing with her mouth wide open. Checking the room again before his arrival, her glance fell on this photo, which she put away in a drawer. Her sister was engaged. She went out often.

Rachel had dinner with him. They spent the evening together, and he returned home.

He thought the house was unusual. A little tower rose from the tile roof. The door was never locked. He would knock and then enter. You entered directly into the dining room which was never used. You reached the little tower from the adjacent kitchen, a big wooden door in the back wall opened onto a stair. On the second floor you could see a row of unused rooms suffused with light filtering between the slats of the closed shutters. You couldn't set foot in there, stones could fall. There was no bathroom. She boiled water in a basin and washed in the kitchen sink. The shabbiness of the house was obvious. He didn't speak of it. He told her about Paris, he stressed his attachment to the city, the impossibility for him of living anywhere else. He described where he lived.

Not far from the Arc de Triomphe.

Boulevard Pereire, in a building set back from the street behind the garden.

Two apartments on the same floor. One occupied by his parents, where he still had his bedroom, the other occupied by his brother, his brother's wife, and their two daughters.

When he talked about his brother's wife, he said "she's a short, simple girl." And to explain his brother's choice, "all he wanted was for her to be kind," in a tone that let you suppose he had probably married beneath him.

At the time, young men were doing their military service in Algeria. Her sister was engaged to a boy who had just spent two years there, he'd returned with memories of the horrors. As a student, my father had benefited from a deferment, and then later on he had been called up and was supposed to have left immediately. But through a friend whose lover he had been and whose father was a cabinet minister, he had been posted to Germany, he was a secretary, an interpreter, and a driver for an officer. One evening, returning to the barracks by car, a girl had stood him up, he was angry, he was driving fast. He struck a pedestrian. The man bounced off the hood, the body was thrown onto the road, he didn't stop. The man was found the next day, dead. There was an investigation, the description of the car was given, my father was incarcerated. So when he arrived at Châteauroux he was just out of military prison.

A song by Eddie Constantine, "Cigarettes, whisky et p'tites pépées," was playing on the radio, a very popular song, they were in bed, everything was going well. All of a sudden his face clouded over.

"What's the matter, Pierre, something wrong?"

"I don't know if I can speak to you about this... I think I can. There are no secrets between us, right, Rachel?"

"I hope not."

"You won't judge me, you won't tell anyone?"

"Pierre, do you know what my colleagues say about me at the office?"

"What do they say?"

"Mlle Schwartz is as silent as the grave!"

"Well ..." The words emerged from his throat slowly, like from a knot being loosened. "Well, that song."

"Yes."

"Cigarettes, whisky et p'tites pépées ..."

"Yes ..."

"Well ..."

"Pierre, I won't say anything."

"The first time I heard it ... I was in prison."

"In prison, how come?"

"In military prison, during my service. It's the first time I've spoken of it."

"I won't say anything, don't worry."

"I was scared. Instead of stopping ... well, I sped up."

"..."

"You know, I'm an unhappy man, Rachel. I'm a lonely person. I have no friends. Everyone has rejected me. All around me was a pack of hounds, you understand, a pack of hounds, and me isolated in the middle ..."

She brought her pillow closer to his, she laid her head on his torso, put her arm across his stomach, and pressed herself against him.

"Were you in prison a long time?"

"A year and a half. I escaped. But everyone was on my tail. I was recaptured immediately. No one helped me. It was horrible. My father wrote every day, fortunately. He at least didn't judge me."

Her cheek on his chest, she could hear his heart beating.

"I was proud. I was authoritarian. I was abrupt. I always had to lord it over the others. Show my superiority. I was a vain little young man, you know. A sort of little marquis, quite pretentious. Not very likeable. I don't want to be that man anymore." His expression was totally sincere. "When that fellow crossed the road, I had absolutely no control. I didn't have time to brake and I panicked. It happened like that because I was angry. From pride. From vanity. That's not too brilliant, is it? I'm not that man anymore, Rachel."

He was speaking of himself in the past. He said he wanted to change. He was in bed looking up at the ceiling. Then he turned his face to her and sucked on her lips. He put his hand back under the sheets. Inserted a finger into her vagina. Pushed it in. Then he entered her. She had a complex sensation. An electric current flowed across her on the surface, at the same time the wave reached the depths of her being. She had the impression of being annihilated. It was a happy impression, one of being a human being but not necessarily herself. A human being, anyone at all, a mortal. She had never experienced that. She climaxed as much from the comings and goings of his phallus as from the fact that she could feel herself: both captured as a thing in a great void and integrated into this nothingness; included. It was a sensation of truth. She didn't have the banal feeling of being filled, but of being annihilated, emptied of her personality, reduced to dust. Her very matter transformed, her person chemically modified. She was a part of this nothing. The time to which she belonged had suddenly stretched to millions of years. Her body stiffened for a few seconds, the time of a moan, then she turned her head on the pillow. She cried. He accelerated the movement and ejaculated on her stomach, out of precaution, as he always did, and according to the agreement they had.

They went to sleep. She woke up a few minutes later. She had to go home.

"What time is it? It's late, it is."

"Don't say *it is*."

"I know. But when it's spoken language … one can …"

"Do you say 'it ain't raining'? Or do you say 'it isn't raining'?"

"It *isn't* raining."

"Your sister says 'it ain't raining,' have you noticed? You ought to tell her, socially she'll be penalized. A guy can go to school as long as he wants, if he says *it ain't raining*, maybe he'll have his diploma, but that's all."

"You know, Didi …"

"She doesn't care, is that it? And you? You don't care either?"

"No. I care."

The first time they spent the whole night together, the next morning, when she opened her eyes, he was already awake. He was looking at her.

"It's wonderful, Rachel."

He caressed her cheek.

"Something's happening with us, you know."

"I think so."

"If it weren't for your eyes, this wouldn't be happening, do you know that? They are so beautiful, your beautiful green eyes. A green so soft … You are a very pretty woman, Rachel. You know that, don't you?"

"Let's see … Do I know it? I don't think so. Not necessarily, no."

"You are really a very beautiful woman."

"Thank you."

"You have a very beautiful body. You could have very handsome men."

"You're the one I want to please, I find you very handsome." She mentioned actors whom she would like less than him. "You have charm, it's more interesting, you are more than handsome."

He laughed. "You're sweet, big girl. We're good together, aren't we, Rachel?"

"Anyhow, I'm good with you."

"I know you are good. I feel it under my hand. And here, in the hollow of my arm. And here, between my lips. Here too. And here."

"I've never been like this with anybody, Pierre."

"Rachel …"

"Yes."

"Tell me we will always be like this. Like in this moment. That nothing will destroy this, ever. Tell me nothing will change between us. That in a month we will be exactly like here. How we are here. With your legs between mine. That we'll feel what we feel at this moment. This exact impression that we have here, at this instant, both of us, that we are one person. Tell me that, Rachel. Say, *Yes, Pierre*."

She closed her eyes.

"Tell me. Look at me."

"Yes, Pierre. I would like this to continue, too, you know. As long as possible, not just for another month."

He asked questions about how she saw her life. "Do you see your life in Châteauroux? Or would you like to leave and live somewhere else?"

"I don't know yet. I can leave."

"Do you want to get married?"

"I don't know. What about you?"

"Me?... Me, no. I want to be able to do what I want."

"You couldn't if you were married?"

"Certainly not."

"Why? Because you couldn't have mistresses?"

"Yes, but not only that. With someone like you, in any case, I wouldn't be able to do what I want."

"Why do you say that?"

"Because you are very demanding, Rachel. Because you like to impose yourself. For people to pay attention to you, including sexually. If I let you, you'd direct operations, wouldn't you?"

"Not at all. Why do you say that?"

"You don't let yourself go!"

"It can happen, yes, I'm wary sometimes, but ... Maybe at the beginning. When I didn't know you yet. But now, less and less. Does that bother you?"

"For a woman to trust is important."

"I trust you, Pierre. I don't think I'm someone who directs. On the contrary."

"Kiss me. Come. You don't know what I like to appreciate about you! Do you? And what I like less. Let me handle it, okay?"

"I like it when you take the initiative ... That's what I like with you."

"Come here, big girl. Come on, come. Don't worry. Give me a smile." He caressed her back through the sheet as if his hand was immense and had the power, just by gliding across the fabric, to make her shiver from the small of her back to the nape of her neck.

"Ahh. That's good, Pierre. I love it."

"If you came to live in Paris, we could see each other often. Would you like to?"

"Of course. But what about my work?"

"You can work in Paris, can't you?"

"I would have to ask for a transfer …"

"I could help you find a little apartment. And if you want to get married, because I understand, for a woman it's important, I wouldn't object."

"With another man, you mean?"

"Oh yes. I told you, for me it's not possible. That would change nothing for us. We could see each other as much as you like."

"You wouldn't be jealous?"

"No." Then he slapped the tips of her breasts, as if distracted. He told her to concentrate and to climax like that. She buried her head in the pillow, eyes closed. Then the back of her neck rose up, stiffened. She gave a sigh, and her head again became heavy. She remained lying down a few seconds. Then she sat up in the bed. And she took his member in her hand.

"Have you had a lot of lovers?"

"No. Just one before you. But I was engaged. When I was very young …"

"Tell … Was he a good catch?"

"Not bad, yes. But I was very young. I was sixteen."

"He was the one, your first lover?"

"No, this one was my fiancé. His name was Charlie."

"With a y, was he an American, your Charly?"

"No, a Frenchman. And he was very respectful of the young

girl I was. We were engaged for two years. He was a very sweet boy. He would have brought me the moon!"

"What did he do, your boyfriend Charlie?"

"He had to finish his education. He was very young too. He was going to take over his father's dental prosthesis business. His parents lived in Paris, in the sixteenth arrondissement."

"Where?"

"Quai Louis Blériot."

"Why didn't it work out?"

"The date for the wedding was about to be set. We were writing each other. My father had even gone to see his family in Paris. And then I had had enough."

"You're the one who broke it off?"

"Yes, I stopped answering his letters. Brutally. Just like that. Without really thinking."

"Poor guy."

"And he did suffer. But I don't think I realized it, I was so young. He waited for me. But in the end he got married."

"Poor guy."

"He wrote Mama to find out if I was receiving his letters."

"Do you regret it?"

"Hmm … Yesss … Sometimes. Occasionally. He offered me a life … how shall I put it? Well, sometimes it would occur to me that I would have had a more comfortable life, for sure. I wouldn't be going to the Sécu each morning, you see, for example." She laughed.

Girls at the time dreamed of marrying someone who would allow them to stay home. To not be obliged to work.

"Why did you give up the chance to marry him?"

"I didn't like him."

"Meaning?"

"I didn't like it when he kissed me."

Physically, my father didn't fit the tastes of the period. People liked tall men with crewcuts. He was of average height, rather thin, very myopic, he had slightly bulging eyes, thick eyeglasses, and he didn't care about sartorial elegance. But he had charm, assurance, a smile, which made other men no longer exist for her. Those who saw them walking hand in hand saw a very beautiful young woman accompanied by a man of no interest. He had a way of carrying his head and a way of moving his shoulders when he walked that made him absolutely unique in her view. Her female friends didn't understand what she saw in him. Their incomprehension amused her. She was alone in understanding his allure. His charisma, his way with words. So she was exiled in the city. But she had at last found someone who made sense to her.

Nicole lived alone with her mother in a little apartment along the boulevards. She was a brunette with curly hair, her voice was high pitched, discordant but seductive. They had known each other for a long time. They both worked at the Sécurité Sociale, the offices of which had just been transferred to Rue Jacques Sadron. They saw each other often.

"What are you going to do when he returns to Paris?"

"He asked me if I would consider leaving Châteauroux."

"He wants you to leave with him?"

"Not really with him. He wants us to continue living like we do here, I think. He insists a lot on his independence."

"And you, what do you think about it?"

"I don't know. We're good together."

"That's for sure, Rachel. Even I can see it. You're good, you're happy, it's obvious, it really is."

"Really! You think so? Is it so visible? How can you see it?"

"I couldn't say. One can just see that you're good together. He's attentive, he's present, he's nice with you. He's always looking at you …"

"I don't think we would see each other every day if he didn't love me … Anyhow we love each other."

"Do you get the feeling he'd like to get married?"

"I don't think so. He says he wants to remain free. But we talked about having a child."

"Wait a sec, he wants you to leave Châteauroux, he wants a child, but he doesn't want to get married? Isn't that bizarre?"

"That's how he is. He is very attached to his freedom. He's not an ordinary guy, that's for sure. But we love each other. That's for sure too, and he wants a child with me. That would be so good."

"If he wants a child with you, that means he pictures a future with you. He's a good man, he's intelligent, he knows what he's doing. He's thoughtful, he's not someone who messes around. He's attentive, he's sensitive. He's not an arrogant type, even though he could be."

He was courteous in society. He took an interest in people, he asked them questions, he listened to them. Nicole appreciated that.

"I suppose you like him physically?"

"Of course. And we are good together. We are good together. That's how it is, what do you want me to say … We. Are. Good. Together."

Early in the spring, they spent a weekend in the Creuse region. They had known each other for six months. They slept in a little hotel in Crozant. The weekend was wonderful. He had rented a car, they went to Gargilesse and to Nohant. They visited the home of George Sand. There were documents about her life, about her lovers, details about those who had spent time at Nohant, about her novels, what had inspired what, the things she saw from her windows, the places where certain scenes from her books were situated, the painting where she is dressed like a man in a suit, jacket, pants, shirt, floppy necktie, her fingers holding a cigar.

"Anyhow, at work, one day a woman arrived wearing pants – she was a funny one – it wasn't like George Sand. Right away she was called in by the boss. And he requested that she go change."

"You don't have the right to go to work in pants?"

"Oh no! Certainly not. No, no. I went to see him, that boss! I told him I didn't think it was right that she had been sent home. It wasn't very serious, after all, for that one time."

"Was it important to you?"

"Yes, it was important. Especially because that man took liberties! In the beginning he wanted me to be his mistress. And since I never gave him a chance, he made life hell for me for years. Fortunately he put me in a different department and I'm not his personal secretary anymore."

"He doesn't know you aren't interested in little bosses of his type?"

"Exactly! Apparently not."

On the way back, they took photos of themselves in the country. She took a photo of him, and he took the same photo of her. Leaning on the same post, in the same position. The one and the other both taken from far away. She had on a short-sleeved sweater, tapered pants, ballet shoes, and a scarf around her neck. He a white shirt with the sleeves rolled up and belted pants loose around his hips. You couldn't make out their features very well. You could see the position of their bodies, the frame, and the surrounding countryside.

It started to rain, they got back in the car. On the drive home, they talked about the places where they dreamed of going one day.

"I have a passion that I absolutely have to satisfy each year, if only for a few days: Italy."

"I've never been."

"You absolutely must go."

The car crossed villages she had always known. He pronounced the names on the signs they passed and explained their etymology. The houses filed past. The light rain that fell on the windshield began to turn heavy. The sky was uniformly gray.

"Your father – is he someone you admire, Rachel?"

"I must have admired him, yes, I suppose. But I can't say I love him."

"Why?"

"Why? Ah. That's hard to say." She paused. Then: "Well, let's say …" She took the time to think each word: "Well, let's say … He's someone who rejected me."

"Why do you say that?"

"He left when I was four and didn't return until I was seventeen. During those thirteen years he was away, I had a photo of him that I looked at every day. It had been taken in the lane, he was smoking a pipe, he had on a fine Prince-of-Wales overcoat. I found him elegant. When I was angry with Mama, I would look at this photo, 'Oh man,' I would say to myself, 'if only my father were here, he at least would understand me.' And then …"

There were a few seconds of silence.

"Why are you stopping? Continue."

"I don't like to talk about it. It makes me feel bad."

"You can't drive him out of your life."

"I know that."

"He's your father."

"I know. Okay. I'm going to try to tell you. When he came back after thirteen years, he had been absent the whole time of the war …"

"How much later did he come back?"

"A year or two. I was still very thin, we had had lots of shortages. And we didn't start eating again immediately after the war. We had had deprivations for a long time. I suppose I was not a very pretty girl. I think I didn't flatter his vanity. One day, he called me into the garden. And … Actually, I don't know if I want to continue."

He let go of the steering wheel, he put a hand on her knee. "Continue."

"Well I didn't know him, you see, when he returned. I was

expecting a lot from him. Too much, probably. And one day, we had just finished lunch, he told me to follow him. And he went out into the garden … And in a path in the garden, he began to compare me to his brother's children."

She changed the position of her body, like someone getting ready to tell an anecdote that's going to be somewhat long. "And he put his hands like this – like this, you see?" She put her hands facing each other, parallel. There was a space of about twenty centimeters between them. "Like that, face to face. And to show the distinction between me on the one side and his brother's children on the other, he moved his hands like this, from one side of the garden to the other."

She moved her hands to the right. "So on the one side there were his brother's children. Who were, let's say, 'well behaved.'" She held her hands in the air for a second. Her palms facing each other, her arms partially extended toward the outside, toward the window of the car. "And on the other, me." She moved her hands toward the steering wheel.

She seemed hesitant to continue. Then she started moving her parallel hands back and forth. As if from one side of the garden to the other. Toward the wheel. Toward the window.

"So … his brother's children were beautiful, intelligent, cultivated. On one side. And I was ugly, stupid, ignorant. On the other. It continued like that all the way down to the river. The garden is long, you know. I was just there, I wasn't saying anything."

She imitated the chopped-up pronunciation of her father: "Your cousins are beautiful. You are ugly! They are intelligent. You are stupid! They are educated. You are ignorant!"

"What's his background, exactly? What's that accent you're putting on?"

"Oh, I don't know if I'm putting on a particular accent. His parents came from Eastern Europe, he was born in Egypt, in Alexandria. He had an Italian passport. He started traveling very early. He learned international accounting. I suppose he spoke with an oriental accent. Or it was a mixture of all that – Romanian, Hungarian, Hebrew, Arabic, Italian, I don't know. And he ended his gesture like this, with a little rebound. Like this, you see …"

In an abrupt move, she threw her hands up. "Once we were in front of the river, he said to me: 'In conclusion, I would be ashamed to introduce you to my mother.'"

Her features were contracted, all expression had been eliminated from her face. There remained a sort of coldness that could have passed for placidity. "And I said nothing to my mother, when we went in."

Once more, my father put his hand on her knee, he caressed her thigh through the cloth of the tapered pants.

"What's your relationship like now?"

"Well, he comes to Châteauroux every once in a while. It's complicated, because he doesn't know that Didi exists, so when he arrives she leaves. Mama never told him she had had another child … And in the neighborhood everyone held their tongue. Nobody ever said anything to him."

"Not even you?"

"Oh no. It's Mama's secret. She had Didi with a man who died just before the end of the war. I never really knew who it was. Neither did Didi."

"Does he have money, your father?"

"He has bank accounts, according to what he says. In Italy, Switzerland, Israel, but I have no idea what's in them. Surely not a lot."

"But after all, he's your father, he's not just anybody. Why be disagreeable when he comes two days a year? It wouldn't take much of an effort. You are his only daughter, one day he'll be thinking about his estate …"

"Yes, oh you know, I don't give a damn about that."

"You're wrong, Rachel."

"How about you, your father. Do you admire him?"

"Unlike you, I love my father a great deal. And I admire him a lot. He is an exceptional man. Very intelligent. Curious, brilliant, funny. Very lively, quick. Very cultivated, very sharp, very … He's a most uncommon man. He's very …"

"So he has all the qualities, if I understand correctly …"

"All!" He laughed.

She did too.

"Name some qualities, Rachel ..."

"Oh well, I don't know, let's say ... goodness?"

"Ah! He is extremely good! Extremely!"

They continued to laugh. Their conversation transformed into a game during the last part of the drive. They arrived at Châteauroux, and when he dropped her at the entrance to the lane, they were still at it.

During the months that followed, each time he spoke to her about his father, she gave him his cue: "So now ... How about ... Let's say ... Thoughtfulness!"

And he, with deliberate emphasis: "Ah, extremely thoughtful. He is extremely thoughtful ... He has a thoughtfulness ... Oh, a thoughtfulness ... Extreme."

This little game repeated, their duo became a routine.

"Intelligence?"

"Ah! None more intelligent."

"Generosity?"

"He is ex-treme-ly gen-er-ous. Ex-treme-ly. He is generosity personified. Generosity itself."

He practically never told her about his mother.

When my grandmother returned from Grasse, my mother told her she had met a young man, that he worked at La Martinerie, that she saw him from time to time, that he was nice. Didi was going to be eighteen, she was a warehouse worker at the Quintonine laboratory. Her fiancé was an apprentice cabinetmaker, they were about to be married. The household was preoccupied with a problem: on the day of the wedding, who was going to walk Didi to the altar, since there was no father? My grandmother's uncle offered to. The ceremony was to take place in a country inn. My father was invited. She didn't tell him about the invitation. The songs, the garter, the Berrichon accent, the farandole in the hall, the horseshoe-shaped table, the bow-legged men in their suits, the mail-order dresses, the jokes – she preferred to go without him. Nicole had become a friend of the family. She was seated beside her.

"He has entered my life. For me he is part of my life, I don't see him leaving. You understand? For me, he is in my life. But I don't know how it's going to go. I really don't know."

"You should go see a fortune teller, Rachel. I know one who is really good."

This fortune teller read coffee grounds. After a few seconds, shapes appeared. She identified letters in them, which she commented on. My mother made an appointment. In an ordinary little room, between a sofa and a sideboard, the fortune teller observed the coffee grounds overturned on a plate. The letter P showed. It was particularly important. An upheaval would occur within a horizon of four or five years. A move, a transfer, a death, a shock, something sudden and brutal. But an event would happen that would allow her to overcome this shock. The fortune teller asked her to move the plate again. The coffee grounds inscribed the shape of a C. The image was very hollowed out. The fortune teller was sure of herself, this letter had great importance. Try as she might, my mother couldn't see what this C might correspond to. The fortune teller insisted. The C would count all her life. And it would even be enormously important.

In the middle of spring, the company that employed my father as a translator at La Martinerie informed him his contract would end on April 30. He bought a train ticket for 2:30 in the afternoon on May 2. She asked for the morning off on the 2nd, so they could have a quiet lunch that day.

They spent the 1st together. It was a lot of fun. They went to the forest, they walked on the trails, they went into some underbrush, they ruffled the leaves on principle, since it was the 1st of May, and looked out into the distance without expecting anything. All of a sudden, masses of little white specks appeared before them everywhere. They had chanced upon an exceptional spot. They were walking on the lilies of the valley. They could see other little bells farther off before they had even finished picking what was under their feet. Four hands were not enough. The flowers had a strong scent. They returned to the car with their arms loaded and with the impression they had experienced something unheard-of. Heading back, they stopped for lunch in Chasseneuil.

He was hesitant about ordering oysters, they were available. He decided to wait for Paris. He told her about the Brasserie Lorraine and the Place des Ternes.

"I would really like you to come live in Paris and to keep seeing each other. Will you think about it, Rachel?"

"I would like it too, Pierre. But under what conditions? I don't see myself living in a little room and going to work at the Sécu, with you coming to see me from time to time. Would we do lots of things together? Would you introduce me to your family? Or would there be a complete separation between your life and me?"

"That's not the most important. Is it? In certain areas, there would be separation, yes, of course. But your time would be your own. You are attached to conventions, deep down, that's a difficulty with you, Rachel. I will not marry you, and you know it, we've already talked about that. Come on, smile for me, come, let's go to Rue Grande. We don't have much time left."

A bottle of wine was on the table, uncorked. He inserted a finger into the neck of the bottle, looking at her straight in the eyes, with a smile full of innuendo, moving the finger back and forth inside and outside the bottle, faster or slower. He asked for the bill and they rushed to get into the car.

"No, Pierre, not here."

"Let's get back to Châteauroux right away, then."

"Okay."

He parked on the Descente des Cordeliers, they ran hand in hand to Rue Grande.

"Will you let me come in you today?"

"Yes."

They kissed passionately. She hooked her hands on his neck, on his hair.

"Do you like being a woman?"

"At this moment, yes."

"Why? Tell me why you like being a woman."

"Because I'm with you."

"Is that all?"

"I am yours."

"Is that all?"

"I like what you do to me."

"What do I do to you?"

He placed his palm against her crotch, then pressed a finger into her. "Say, there's a pretty little fountain in there …"

At the office, she worked eight hours a day. The schedule was strict: eight to twelve, two to six. On the 2nd of May, she didn't arrive until three. They had lunch at the Hôtel du Faisan.

"If you want to come to Paris, you'll let me know."

They separated in front of the station.

She headed in the direction of La Caisse. Her mind was blank. She passed in front of the building, she turned left onto Rue Victor Hugo, she crossed the square at the town hall, then took Rue Jacques Sadron. Upon arriving, she called Nicole, who worked at the counter, and she cried into the handset.

Two weeks later she received a letter.

My dear Rachel,

Upon my return to Paris, I spent my first days doing all sorts of errands. As I feared, I arrived too late for the position that I had been offered. But an aviation company proposed an interesting job. After successfully passing an exam, I was accepted. Unfortunately, I learned I would have to go to Toulouse. Naturally I have no desire to be exiled again. For the time being, therefore, I am completely uncertain as to my future.

I would like to know what's happening with you and if your days are spent following the schedule I know or if something has changed. Tell me what you're doing, and what you're feeling.

For me, these days in Paris have had the same effect as usual. I feel

*the presence of something perfect, finished, definitive, that fills me,
and at the same time I have a certain moral anxiety. Imagine a
tight-rope walker who risks falling in any direction at every instant,
but conscious that this risk is his profession and his life.*

Remember me to your little sister.

I kiss your beautiful hands.

Don't forget me.

Pierre

She replied, he wrote again immediately.

My Big Girl,

*Your letter gave me great pleasure. It is so sweet. It made me
happy to recognize your perfume, while regretting that the scent of
your skin wasn't mixed in with it.*

*Resuming good relations with your father is an excellent thing.
Don't stop there. Continue to write him, see him. You should have
applied these same realistic principles and accepted the offer from the
couture house instead of refusing to model. You would have been
generously remunerated. Why couldn't you? Be that as it may, I feel
flattered as well. If you intend to leave Châteauroux, don't neglect to
keep me informed.*

*A little drama occurred here. My mother and my niece had a fall
together, and they had to be hospitalized. Now everything is back to*

normal. But that and many other things make me forget to smile.
And yet with you I was usually cheerful and carefree, wasn't I? I need
your long, soothing hand to slip into mine from time to time. That
would make me feel good.

I am waiting impatiently for a letter from you and, you know, I
see no objection to it being long. On the contrary.

My sweetest thoughts,
Pierre
PS: Thanks for the photo, I love us a lot, too.

She wrote him a few weeks later. They absolutely had to see each
other, she was pregnant.

She received a quick reply: he couldn't come to Châteauroux
before the end of the summer, he needed a vacation, he was going
to Italy.

A few days later, a postcard arrived, mailed from Milan, with
a picture of the cathedral.

Dear Rachel,
After a pleasant stay in Milan, I've now been invited to Rome. I
will probably be back around the 20ᵗʰ, and I hope to be able to see you
soon. This was written on the roof of the cathedral, which takes the
form of a terrace. Keep yourself in good health. It's important.
Pierre

Another card followed, mailed from Rome. It showed the face of the Pietà in black and white.

> Rachel,
> *This is perhaps the most beautiful face in Rome that I'm sending you here. I would like you to feel the same emotion that it gave me.*
> *Write to me: Pensione Ottaviani, via del Tritone 113, Roma.*
> *I'm thinking of you,*
> *Pierre*

He left Italy a few days later. The letter in which he announced his return was written on letterhead from the Marcellin, a hotel in Beaulieu-sur-Mer, he proposed she come spend a week with him there.

> Dear Rachel,
> *My trip to Italy is over. It was full of marvels and instruction. But tiring. That's why, passing through the Côte d'Azur, I decided to stop here to rest for eight or ten days and take a real vacation, à la Hulot. The beginning is very promising. The pension where I'm staying, I could almost say where I've strayed, is populated by old couples straight out of the nineteenth century. It's pot-luck and old fashioned, but basically peaceful. Starting tomorrow: swimming in the sea and tanning sessions. I'm set on returning darkened. Simple*

but healthy plan. I will no doubt be a little bored after a time, but after my touristic emotions in Italy a little dose of boredom can't hurt.

As for you, what are you up to? Why don't you come spend your vacation on the Côte? I couldn't resist the temptation to get to know this region.

Goodbye, Rachel, be well. Kisses.
Pierre

To get to the Côte d'Azur, you have to go through Paris. You arrive at the Austerlitz station and take a train for Nice from the Lyon station. He was waiting for her, he had rented a Renault 4CV. They went directly to Beaulieu-sur-Mer.

It was a wonderful week. They toured the coast. They went everywhere. They had adventures. They were driving on the high corniche from Nice to Menton, admiring the panorama, when all of a sudden the hood popped up. The hood of a 4CV opens from the front and rests against the windshield. They were blinded. Not only was the panorama blocked, but the road – or rather the track between boulders that snaked less than a meter from the precipice – was invisible, and the car was moving. He had good reflexes, he braked slowly. The wheels moved slowly and stopped after a few meters. He got out, slammed the hood solidly shut, and, that great fright behind them, they continued on toward Menton.

At the port, he bought her a little metal brooch, worth nothing but pretty – a seahorse with green eyes.

On the return trip, the train to Paris was packed. They had to stand. The journey took eight or nine hours at the time.

"You can't travel like this in your condition, Rachel."

They got out at Saint-Raphaël.

Since he hadn't worked for several months, and it was the end of vacation, and he had spent a lot in Italy, and he never asked his father for money, he had nothing left. The last night in Nice, at the Palais de la Méditerranée, he had wanted to gamble, she lent him her last fifty-franc bill, he lost, she didn't have anything left either.

They looked for a savings bank, the Caisse d'Épargne, and he took out a hundred francs from his account, and they reserved seats for the next day.

They had an additional evening of vacation. They dined in a fine restaurant. And spent their last night in a pretty little hotel facing the sea.

On the train, they had a last conversation.

"If you had been rich, I would surely have thought about it."

"Oh really …"

"I would have thought about it. Yes. It's true. I am being frank. With you I've always been frank. I won't marry you, I have always said so. And … we agreed about having this child."

"Yes."

"You are pregnant, but that effectively changes nothing, Rachel. Right? We had spoken about it, hadn't we?"

"Yes, yes."

He reiterated the proposal he had made upon leaving Châteauroux, on May 2: "Ask for your transfer. I'll help you find a room or a little apartment."

"I'll think about it, Pierre. I promise."

"Think, and let me know."

"I'll give you my reply before the end of the month."

It was the last days of June.

They said goodbye on the platform of the Austerlitz station. The coaches were almost empty, she was alone in her compartment. A little sad. Not excessively. She had always known, deep down, that it couldn't happen otherwise.

Arriving in Châteauroux, she took the Avenue de la Gare, and on the way to the Rue de l'Indre, things began to take shape. First, she was going to tell her mother that she was pregnant. And if her mother agreed, she would stay. They both sat down at the kitchen table. After an hour's conversation, the decision was made. She would stay.

But, contrary to what had been decided on the platform of the Austerlitz station, she didn't inform my father of her decision. She told Nicole: "No, I didn't write him. I broke up with him."

In October, a short letter arrived in the mail. A few lines in the familiar handwriting with minuscule letters and outsized down-strokes.

Dear Rachel,
Don't think I have forgotten to reimburse what I owe you. But since vacation, my financial situation is verging on bankruptcy and is improving only at a despairingly slow rate. I have not yet been able to return to my father a penny of the 80,000 francs he lent me. And while my brother is still not in a position to settle what he borrowed from me, the tax man has taken an interest in me. And at present I make less than what I had been led to hope for, about 20,000 francs less than in Châteauroux.
I would not like you to hold it against me for delaying the reimbursement of the amount you advanced me at Nice at the Palais de la Méditerranée. I couldn't do it earlier, I hope nevertheless that you never doubted I would do it.
Goodnight, Rachel.
Pierre

That was all.

The note was accompanied by a fifty-franc bill.

She regretted not having kept him up to date about her decision. She thought she had behaved badly. That she was partly responsible for the turn of events. A dry note accompanied by a fifty-franc bill as reimbursement for the amount she had advanced him to gamble at the Palais de la Méditerranée.

She was going to be alone through the coming months, giving birth, and probably declaring the child. The social worker at the Caisse de Sécurité Sociale was a friend of hers. She knew of cases where the man didn't want to deal with the woman but wanted the child. While she was immobilized at the hospital, he would go to city hall, recognize the child, the man's wife became the official mother. To counter this kind of situation, a law had just been passed. These were the very first dispositions on behalf of children born to unmarried couples. The law allowed the mother to recognize the child before its birth through a two-part procedure. One had to go to city hall armed with a certification of pregnancy and return after the delivery with the certificate from the hospital, to specify the sex, the first name, and the date of birth.

She was five months' pregnant and had already put on a lot of weight. The employee on duty was about forty, a plaque with his name, Georges Piat, sat on the counter, she told him she wished to take advantage of a new procedure called "Recognition before birth." He took a form, inserted it into a typewriter, asked a few questions, then turned the platen with the sound of a cricket, and drew the sheet out of the typewriter. He signed it. He looked up at her and gave it to her without a word.

The paper was titled "Birth" and it stipulated: "On October 20, 1958, 3:45pm, Rachel Schwartz, secretary, born in Châteauroux on November 8, 1931, domiciled in Châteauroux, Indre, Chemin des Prés-Brault, declared to Us to recognize her child, the child which she, Rachel Schwartz, declares to be presently pregnant with. Having read it, the declarer signed with Us, Georges Piat, Head Clerk, Registrar of Vital Records in Châteauroux, by delegation from the Mayor."

At the bottom was the signature of the employee, his name, his position, and in the margin a number, the name of my mother, and the name of the procedure.

Around the same time, she heard about a clinic and a well-reputed doctor who practiced there. Only preparations for the birth and deliveries were done there. This clinic was on the Route d'Argenton. She decided she would give birth there. A neighbor who lived in the lane, M. Ligot, told her, "When you need me, let me know," because he had a car. She felt the first pains one evening around eleven, her mother went to get him. He drove them to the clinic. They admitted her to a room. She had contractions, everything was happening normally. They took her to the labor room. The doctor was there. Everything was going well. But at one point the contractions stopped.

It might have been a psychological reaction, which could be explained by the way the last months had gone. The birth had become complicated. It was too late to do a caesarian, because I was too far advanced. And she was no longer having contractions.

Thirty minutes was too long, the time to prepare the caesarian, I would die. The doctor decided to use forceps. She had had contractions all night, I was in danger. She had to be put to sleep very quickly. What would come next was going to be delicate. My head was engaged, and she was sleeping. They had to insert the forceps without touching me, being careful with my head.

When she woke up, while she was still under the haze of the anesthesia, my grandmother came to her: "You have a beautiful little girl."

They brought me to her so she could see me. Not for long, she was still in a fog. They took me back to the nursery. The midwife put a hand on her shoulder and told her: "The doctor did an extraordinary job."

She left to let her rest in the room, watched by a nurse. When she returned, she could see right away that things were not good. My mother was very pale. She was having an internal hemorrhage. She was on the verge of passing. The nurse hadn't realized a thing. The doctor was called back. They gave her emergency transfusions. They did the first one with universal blood. Then they tested her blood group and gave her a second one.

The next day I was in the room with her. She was thankful she had chosen this clinic rather than the hospital, which did not have a good reputation. We wouldn't have survived, either one of us. She stayed for about ten days. My grandmother came to see us every day. My uncle and my aunt also came. All our friends came.

When she returned home, my grandmother had bought some mimosa, a vase overflowed with it, light yellow, on the kitchen sideboard. The scent was intoxicating. She sat facing the window, I was in her arms.

Nicole came to see her in the afternoon. "You know, Nicole ... just now I was here, sitting on this chair, I had Christine in my arms, I was looking outside. And I thought: So now what?"

A few days later, she wrote to my father asking him to come see me. He couldn't, he sent her a telegram: "Regrets, materially impossible come today, Pierre."

He came in July. I was five months old. He came for the day and left the same afternoon. I was in my cradle.

Before he left, she told him: "It would be good if you recognized Christine."

"I'll think about it. I'll tell you."

Not having any word after a few weeks, she wrote again. Her letter came back marked "No longer at this address."

She took the train to Paris. Early in the afternoon, she went to the desk in the lobby of the Michelin building. It was the only address she had. She asked to speak to the director and was sent to the top floor. They ushered her into an office.

A man of medium height, clearly a man of responsibilities, pointed to a little armchair.

"Please, Mademoiselle."

"Your son and I have a little girl."

He was aware of it. His son had told him he didn't feel responsible.

"I can't tell you much. I am a father!"

The remainder of the discussion unfolded smoothly. He spoke to her quite calmly.

A few weeks later, she received a letter from Strasbourg – on the envelope, the fine letters with overly long downstrokes: Mademoiselle Rachel Schwartz, Chemin des Prés, Rue de l'Indre, Châteauroux.

It was a letter of a few lines, and he gave her his new address. When my uncle took a pretty photo of me, she would send it to him. One of them was taken at the edge of a pond. I was smiling. I had on a straw hat that belonged to him, too big for me.

∾

The summer I was two years old, she decided we would go to a little hotel in Arcachon. She wrote to him, proposing that he should come spend the weekend of July 14.

Dear Rachel,

All things considered, particularly the enormous distance, it really will not be possible for me to go to Arcachon. To begin with, I'm apprehensive about a long round trip all by myself, and then, a new factor, I will have some work to finish here during the summer. What I'm doing at the office just never ends, and I can't let things drag on too long, so I'm going to take advantage of the long weekend to make some progress in peace and quiet.

But I'll still be near you in my thoughts. Have a lovely vacation and a pleasant sea breeze!

Pierre

Despite the difficulties a single mother faced back then, all the more so in a little village, she had no regrets. First of all because she had experienced a great passion. She would show me the photo taken of him in the country leaning against a post, and the one of her in the same place and the same position. And I was here, now.

She did not regret having declined his proposal to live in Paris. Retrospectively, she recognized the mistake she had almost made. What would she have done there, alone with me in a little room, with him coming to see her from time to time, not introducing her to his parents, not marrying her, not giving her any stability, any protection, any social situation – when she was in an unknown place, without help, without support?

Before I was born, she had begun to correct everyone who called her Mademoiselle. Since my birth, everyone, or almost everyone, called her Madame Schwartz.

She thought I was a bit nervous, but sensitive, sweet, and affectionate. My happiness was visible. My uncle photographed me astride a rocking swan placed on the kitchen table. Because I had hit my nose several times on its wooden neck, my grandmother had concocted a stuffed cushion to dampen the blows. I rocked energetically, and I would burst out laughing. The photo was sent to my father.

At age three, I would go to the grocer's all by myself and would circulate freely within the confines of a few streets. Neighbors would encounter me in the lane. They would ask me to sing a song, to dance the twist, I didn't need music. There were other children my age in the neighborhood. Nathalie Olejnik lived at 38 Rue de l'Indre, right beside the archway people passed under to enter the lane. I went to her house every day. I would leave before her father came home.

"Really, Christine, Mr. Olejnik is very nice."

"I know, Nana, but I'm scared."

"You have no reason to be afraid, there's no danger."

"Yes, but I'm scared of fathers."

"You shouldn't be, Christine."

"I know, Nana, but I'd rather leave before he arrives."

Chantal Ligot lived across the street. There were rabbits and chicks at her house. To get there, I just had to cross the lane.

In the evening, we had dinner in the kitchen. Sometimes, in the middle of the meal, I would suddenly get up. I would go around the table, kiss my mother, then my grandmother, or the reverse. I would hug them. And sit down again. I adored my grandmother. I loved my mother.

"More than infinity."

As soon as I learned how to write, I wrote poems about her beauty. And about the feelings I had. I planned trips with her, and I drew plans for the ideal house where we would live when I was grown up.

I wasn't allowed to leave the table before the end of the meal. One day friends were waiting for me outside. A banana was lying on my plate, I didn't want it. She insisted. I left the table and threw the banana across the room. It landed on the other side of the kitchen.

"Christine, you will pick up that banana."

She got up and stood in front of the banana.

"Christine, you will pick up this banana."

Her tone was firm. She was standing straight.

"You will pick up this banana, Christine."

I had my eyes fixed on the floor. She looked at me, articulated:

"Christine. You will pick up this banana!"

She repeated the sentence, lengthening the silences. Staring me down. My grandmother said nothing. I left the kitchen and went into my room. I came back with my doll in my arms. I stood in front of the banana.

"Pick up the banana, doll."

I insisted.

Then I relented: "You don't want to pick up the banana, doll? Ah well, Christine will pick it up."

I left.

Alone in the kitchen, they burst into laughter.

Another time I refused to eat my soup. I had put my elbows on the table and my head between my hands. I rocked my head from left to right, leaning on alternating elbows.

"Ooh God, I'm so fed up, my God, really I'm fed up, I'm fed up, I'm fed up, really I'm fed up!... Really I'm fed up, so fed up, I'm so fed up, fed up, fed up, fed up! I'm fed up, I'm fed up, I'm fed up, I'm so fed up, I'm so fed up, my God …"

They exchanged glances and waited for me to go out before commenting.

Since I liked red, my grandmother knitted me red sweaters, red scarves. Sometimes to please me my mother dressed me entirely in red. We went to a bakery one day, I was wearing a little red coat and red pants, people asked me if I was Little Red Riding Hood. I replied, there was a little conversation, we left once we were served. The door was closing behind us, and as it was almost done turning on its hinges someone inside said, "What a darling little boy."

"It's easy to see I'm a girl, Mama, they're stupid, those people."

We were outside.

"They didn't look carefully. You're wearing pants, your hair is short."

"But still! Even if I'm in pants and short hair. They're stupid."

Rectifying was not feasible, the door had just closed. We were walking. We were leaving.

"They didn't look carefully, that's all. They were working."

"Little Red Riding Hood was a girl, anyway. They know *that*."

Some things made my blood boil. Like that. But they didn't bother her. I kept on walking beside her, holding her hand. I would not have thought of taking my hand away.

Sometimes I would decide to run ahead of her. I would get ahead by a few meters, then turn around and charge toward her so she would catch me. She would take me in her arms, raise me up, and spin me around.

"Wooooooooooo ... Wooooooooooo ... Wooooooooooo ..."

It didn't mean anything. It accompanied the rhythm of her steps, turning in place.

If I did a bad thing, she would explain to me why I deserved a punishment. She was going to give me a spanking. I offered my rear end. And she administered it. Then I said I was sorry and kissed her.

For Christmas when I was three, she gave me a little red tricycle. I rode it in the lane and in the garden. They could see me pedaling from the window. One day, I was pedaling down the path in the garden, I had on a little red skirt, she watched me from time to time. At one point, she could no longer see me. Carried away by the rhythm of my feet on the pedals, I wasn't able to brake. I fell into the river. She heard shouting. She came running. I was right at the end of the path. I'd gotten out of the river, I was holding my bike. I was drenched. My skirt was dripping. And I was screaming:

"I fell into the water I fell into the water I fell into the water I fell into the water I fell into the water I fell into the water I fell into the water I . . ."

Ad libitum unable to stop, and sobbing.

She dried me and put me into her bed with two fat pillows behind my back.

We spent our Sundays with my uncle, my aunt, and my cousins. In Bellebouche, about thirty kilometers from Châteauroux, a pond had been built. We went there as soon as the weather turned warm. We swam, we had fun. My uncle, grabbing a wrist and an ankle, spun me around like an airplane in the sky, climbing, descending, hovering. We returned home after nightfall. In autumn we went to the Poinçonnet Forest. We played hide-and-seek in the underbrush, gathered acorns, dead leaves, moss. Or we went to the public gardens. We took the shortcut that went from our house to the lower gate of the gardens. There was a little stream with a ford. I crossed it hopping from stone to stone, my cousin followed. A path bordered by chestnut trees led to the swings. One day, in spite of being warned, I ran under them. One of the swings hit me on my eyebrow. Blood started to flow. Possibly I had put my eye out. She came running. My uncle panicked at the sight of all the blood spurting out. Looking for a doctor, he carried me in his arms toward the other exit of the public gardens, the one that opened onto Avenue de Déols. Just before that he had taken a photograph. I was wearing a little skirt with suspenders and a mohair vest.

When my uncle photographed something, he liked to have a perspective, something in the background, flowers, a landscape, a vista behind the person, the group, the moment he was immortalizing. Many photos were taken in the lane. Chantal Ligot on a rocking horse, my cousins, my little friend Jean-Pierre who wheeled me around in a wheelbarrow, me riding my bike. Others were taken in the courtyard. One of a little rattan chair just my size, in which my doll was sitting. I was pictured leaning over her, standing, attentive, my grandmother was behind me touching a lilac leaf.

Almost all women stopped working after they got married or when they had their first child. They were waiting at the school when it let out in the afternoon. My mother was one of the few who weren't there, she left her office too late. I went home all by myself, taking a little side-street to the right of the school. Then I took the Descente des Cordeliers, a paved street that curved down and crossed Rue de l'Indre. At the crossing, I would stop. I'd sit down at the corner. I'd play with the slugs. I'd unstick the snails that were suctioned onto the pavement, crouched, attentive, absorbed by what I was doing, under a fine mist that was falling. And then I went on. Looking down along my entire height, I contemplated the polished black shoes she had bought me. I went down Rue de l'Indre to number 36, I passed under the archway, and I entered the lane.

"Hello, Christine! Did you work hard at school today?"

In the lane, there were a lot of people. Neighbors who said hello. Passers-by. The area had not yet been renovated. You would see women washing their linen in the washtubs.

From the top of the stairs of the house, I observed the comings and goings. My grandmother was often in a rest home or in the hospital. When she was home, most of the time she was lying down. I sat at the top of the stairs. I played with my doll. I looked at the garden, the enormous cherry tree, the tomatoes, the iris, the pear tree whose branches hung over the lane. Sometimes a passer-by would pick a pear.

"Say, you there, I'll teach you to steal my pears!"

A little four-year-old girl addressing a stranger, people thought that was funny. The neighbor who saw the scene recounted it to her that evening.

"Well, I'll say, Madame Schwartz, your house is sure being well guarded!"

On Saturdays she didn't work, so she would come when school was out. We would walk through the center of town before going home. We took the Rue Grande. A patisserie sold cookies with hazelnuts, we stopped there. We talked about what had happened during the day. My uncle worked in the Nouvelles Galeries, sometimes we went to see him, we would cross the parking lot at the city hall.

"Look, Mama, a Dauphine, don't you think she looks like she's smiling?"

"I don't know."

"Yes she does! Look, the bumper. It's like a mouth. A laughing mouth. Can you see it? Look. Do you see her teeth?"

"Maybe …"

We agreed about the R8, my uncle's car, it was friendly; and about the Citroen Ami 6, it rocked too much.

"And also, don't you think that 'Ami' is exaggerated, for a name? What do they know about whether I'm their friend?"

"Those are just names they give to cars, you know."

The Citroen DS was Dr. Rosenberg's car, he was the doctor who took care of me.

"I prefer the Ford Taunus, when I'm grown up I'm going to have one."

"I don't know if they'll still be making them then."

"Oh, a Quatre Chevaux, I detest that car. Don't you think it looks mean? Like it's done something evil and it's ashamed. It's looking at us on the sly, don't you think? And besides, it's sad with all that gray."

"That's the car we had, your papa and I, when we spent a week's vacation at Beaulieu-sur-Mer. It was really great to have for our side trips. We went to Nice, Vallauris, Saint-Jean-Cap-Ferrat, Eze, Menton. We did the whole Corniche. It was magnificent. It was an extraordinary week."

She talked to me about him. All children had fathers. Mine was an intellectual. He knew several languages. They had loved each other. It had been a grand love affair. They had wanted me. I was not an accident. She had been proud carrying me for nine months. In spite of the taunts and the words spoken behind her back. Now here I was. She was glad. Where my father was, what he was doing was nobody's business. If people asked me, he was dead, or traveling.

The house was heated by a coal stove in the kitchen. That was all. My grandmother's pulmonary congestion came back. My mother wrote to my grandfather asking him for financial help to install central heating. The reply was mailed from Niger. The illness was just a pretext, he refused. My grandmother's bed was moved into the kitchen. She spent her days on a chaise longue, reading, sewing, or knitting. At night, she sat in bed against raised pillows. In a prone position, with her asthma, she could suffocate.

My mother and I slept in the room beside the kitchen. Her bed was in the middle. Mine under a window from which one could see the moon. At night, we would recite together an Our Father or a Hail Mary. I knelt at the foot of my bed. Then I asked God to protect those whom I loved:

"My mama, my nana, my papa."

After having caressed my cheek, she kissed it. She left the room pulling the door behind her, letting a strip of light filter in.

The break with my father had not been clear-cut. Nothing prevented her from hoping for a reversal. She couldn't accept that "father unknown" was written on my birth certificate. The note was false. Unjust. She hoped it would be corrected. That he would recognize me as his child, that it would be a legal and official act of recognition. She wrote him regularly for this purpose. Her renewed contact had another purpose, to see him again.

Dear Rachel,
At the end of last year, I again changed address and occupation.

From now on you can write to me at 22 Rue du Temple Neuf,
Strasbourg. But I no longer have many opportunities to go to Paris.
  With my best wishes,
  Pierre

He had found a stable and lucrative job working for the European Council. His salary was not taxed, because he was an international functionary. He managed the team of translators of Indo-European languages and carried out certain missions personally.

The summer I was four, she wanted to find a vacation spot that would not be too far from Strasbourg. The Jura or the Vosges.

Dear Rachel,
  I learn from your letter that you will most likely spend your
vacation in the Jura or the Vosges Mountains. If you decide to go to
the Vosges, I advise you to choose the eastern slope, because it will rain
less there. Otherwise, the rainstorms coming from the Atlantic collide
with the western slope, and it often pours for weeks at a time without
stopping. Of course I assume your decision will depend on the replies
you receive from the hotels.
  As for me, I'll take my vacation in the month of June and I'll be
back in Strasbourg around the 8th or 10th of July. If you give me your

address at the hotel, we might be able to see each other. With my best
wishes,

   Pierre

We went to the Vosges, to Gérardmer.

   He came to see us for one day. We took a pedal boat on the
lake. I was happy. I called him Papa. A street photographer took a
photo. I wore a dress with suspenders, a red band in my hair, I was
carrying my doll in my arms. That memory has disappeared from
my recollection. But the photo was enlarged and duplicated.

The following year, she chose the Jura.

   Dear Rachel,
   Your last letter tells me you intend to spend your vacation at
Lons-le-Saulnier, but it doesn't say when. I hope you will find the
time to let me know, and if there is no major hurdle, I shall do my
best to take a trip to the area. A month ago, I passed through
Châteauroux, but in very painful circumstances that didn't allow me
to stop even for a minute, although I thought about it. I was
accompanying my mother to the land of her birth, for her last return.
I couldn't leave the convoy. You were very much with me. And now I
send my best wishes for your health and Christine's.

   Pierre

His mother had killed herself. She had jumped from the fifth floor. My father was in Strasbourg. The rest of the family had just finished lunch in Paris, Boulevard Pereire. They were planning to take a stroll in Parc Monceau. She didn't want to go with them. They had just gone down the stairs and had arrived in the court-yard of the building. They were crossing the courtyard. The body crashed at his brother's feet.

The burial was near Carcassonne. In the village where she was born sixty years earlier. He had just lost his mother; she wrote him a nice letter.

The year I was five, I changed schools. My grandmother was no longer strong enough to make lunch for me, and my school didn't have a cafeteria. The city's private school, Jeanne de France, was on Lafayette Square, they offered lunches, it was right by the house. Châteauroux's notables and the growers of the region who preferred that their children not be schooled in the country put their daughters in that school.

In addition to her asthma and her pulmonary infection, my grandmother became ill with a rather unusual type of tuberculosis, Pott disease, which lodges in the lower back. For treatment the patient must lie flat. Because my grandmother tended to suf-focate when lying flat, treating one illness made the other worse. The care was complicated. She was transferred to the hospital. A few days later, she fell into a coma.

My mother went to see her every evening after leaving the office. She held her inert hand in hers. Sometimes her eyelids trembled. One evening her eyes opened. She saw my mother. She squeezed her hand. She squeezed her fingers very hard, she said:

"Ah! *Ma fille!*"

She'd just had a sudden resurgence of consciousness and energy. Then her hand went limp. She shut her eyes. And she was dead.

Dear Rachel,

The news you send lets me easily imagine how unhappy you must be. But do be convinced, as I am, that your mother has not died altogether. Not that I've converted to the immortality of the soul, but I am certain that you carry within you the impression of her character and her heart. You see, one never dies entirely, because one transmits to others, to those who remain, and especially to those who love you and know you well, a little of one's being. Just as you are astonished to inherit material goods that you knew about without thinking about them, you find yourself in possession of a precious spiritual inheritance, the breadth of which suddenly appears to you. Such at least was the discovery I made upon the death of my mother and is no doubt what you are discovering. When you understand this, the death of those we love is much less sad. It is up to us to give them life beyond their physical disappearance by practicing and transmitting their qualities.

I would have wished to pronounce these words to you in person.

But unfortunately it is absolutely impossible for me to meet you at Lons-le-Saulnier on your dates. It was difficult for me to obtain my vacation in July and now everything has been organized. For the remainder of the summer, my presence in the office is indispensable. The dates cannot be altered. It is really no longer possible for me to change anything at all. We might consider a meeting at some later time, if you like. Unless you can change your times and take your vacation in August. In that case, I will surely be able to take my leave for the necessary time. Write me about this if you see a solution.

Best wishes to you and to Christine,
Pierre

We went to Lons-le-Saulnier in August.

He came to see us for one day. We went for a walk. She was happy. And sad at the moment of departure. *The* departure, with a capital D. Her father's, on the platform of the Châteauroux station. She is four years old. The doors to the cars do not yet close automatically. A traveler can stand in the opening. She is on the platform, looking at the silhouette in the open door. His hand waves. The train pulls away. And recedes into the distance, as the silhouette disappears. Nothing more for thirteen years. Then the silhouette on the same platform. She was seventeen. He got off the train. He took her in his arms, a sob escaped from him as he hugged her.

"Who is this man who sobs while taking me in his arms?"

Of course she knew who he was.

Their mothers' deaths one after the other the same year brought them closer. The day at Lons-le-Saulnier had gone well. The rhythm of their correspondence started up again. Toward the end of the year, she received a letter that ended with "I would like to see you. I am eager to see you."

Dear Rachel,

Your letter pleased me, and be assured I will seize the first chance to come see you. I would like to. I don't understand why you are obliged to leave your dwelling at the Chemin des Prés. But I imagine it won't be long before I know. I'll say it again: I will soon come see you both, as soon as I can, for a very simple reason: I would like to see you. I am eager to see you.

Pierre

It was a short letter, but he'd said: "I would like to see you. I am eager to see you." Things were evolving. People changed, he had lost his mother, he had matured. In her bed at night, when her eyes were closed, the sentences rocked her to sleep: "I would like to see you. I am eager to see you." And at the same time kept her from sleeping.

She received a second letter a few days later. He announced his arrival at the end of the month or the beginning of the next. Probably a Sunday. The sentences ran through her mind: "I would like to see you. I am eager to see you." One didn't write that without meaning it. The plural "you" was not indifferent. "I would like to see *you both*." Was he going to recognize me? Days passed. The end of the month approached.

She received another letter. It specified the date and time of his arrival.

Dear Rachel,

I will come to Châteauroux on February 13, and I'm planning to stay Sunday. I hope you will be there and I can see you. As for the time of my arrival, it will take place around six or seven in the evening, perhaps earlier. But it is really difficult for me to be more exact. In case of difficulties, you can phone me at 35-34-00 or telegraph or write, of course.

Until then, good health to you both and see you soon.

Pierre

There was a knock on the door. She smiled, happy. There he was.

"It's your papa."

I had just turned six.

"Oh come on, Christine, you do know him. You saw him at

Gérardmer when you were very little. Don't you remember we did some pedal-boating?...Well, that was with your papa."

The three of us had dinner. When I was in bed, they had a discussion.

"I have something to tell you."

"Yes …"

"I am married." He described his wife. "Blonde. Average height. Blue eyes. Very beautiful hair. She's German. Very young. Born in Hamburg. Her father is a doctor. She is pregnant, we had to get married very quickly. I am going to have a child. I wasn't thinking of marrying her, you know my way of thinking. But her father was very convincing, and actually I am very happy. Particularly about marrying a German."

"Why?"

"They are the only women, besides Japanese women, who really like to look after men. So many men were killed in Germany during the war. The German women wait on them hand and foot. And her father was very insistent. That counted. Okay, they are quite well off. It's a cultivated family. They are pleasant people. Great music lovers, like all Germans of a certain level. They're of gentility, as they say."

She didn't cry in front of him. Inside, she had fallen apart. She listened to him right to the end with dry eyes. But the effort she was making to let nothing show betrayed her. It hardened her features. He said to her, in a sententious tone: "One day you will wonder how you could have had such feelings about me. And that will be a very sad day!"

Afterward he tried to caress her. She pushed him away. He insisted. He told her he didn't have the same relations with his wife, that he wasn't tender in the same way. She did not give in. It was late. She let him sleep in the house. But early in the morning: "Now you leave!"

She opened the door. I had just got up. He said goodbye to me. He went down the little staircase. We watched him leave from the top of the stairs. He crossed the courtyard. And disappeared down the lane.

Then she collapsed in tears. She cried all the more because the shock was total. How could she have imagined, the day before, that she would find herself in such a state? It was a black hole.

"Come on, we're going to your auntie and uncle's. You and I are not going to stay here."

My aunt and uncle lived a fifteen minutes' walk away. They lived near the center of town, in a neighborhood of housing projects constructed in the early fifties. The streets were empty at that hour on a Sunday. We arrived, took the stairs, my aunt opened the door.

"Is everything okay?"

She was surprised. We were supposed to be busy all weekend.

"Ohhh Didi …"

"What's the matter? What's happened?"

"Ohhh. Didi. Didi. It's hard, Didi." She was panting. She was speaking in short snatches."

"Life is too hard. Too too hard."

"It didn't go well?"

"No, not at all. It didn't go well at all. He's married."

I went to my cousins' bedroom, she followed my aunt into the living room. My uncle was there. She blamed herself. She had imagined things, she had been stupid, she had been naïve. She had believed it. All stemming from two little sentences: "I would like to see you. I am eager to see you." So okay, she had let herself extrapolate.

There was an empty lot behind the building, and in front an esplanade with grass and walkways. Marie-Hélène and I went out to play. We stayed out all morning. We crouched, rubbing little handfuls of dirt between our two palms for a long time, until they fell from our hands like very fine powder. Once we had sifted the dirt to give it this consistency of fine sand, we gathered it up in the hollows of our hands and walked around the lawn looking for buyers, crying: "Who wants soft sand, who wants good fine sand? Who would like my beautiful soft sand? Who will buy my beautiful soft sand?"

Then we went back up to the apartment.

That evening, we stayed for dinner.

We went home after dark.

That was the first time their contact was broken. She had told him, "We have nothing more to do with each other." Then, "Now you leave." He had left. He had brought her an opening onto a world, and she'd had feelings for him that she had never felt before.

The first Priority Urbanization Zones – ZUPs – were being built at the outskirts of the cities. The Cité Saint Jean looked like an American neighborhood; it was situated just beyond the quiet streets that emerged from the boulevards, almost in the country. Our house needed work. She needed to insulate the walls, install a bathroom, and redo the roofing. She couldn't do it. She put it up for sale. A buyer came and, according to him, the value of the house, given its condition, was the garden. He offered a very small sum and she accepted it. She placed a request for housing in the Cité Saint Jean. We went to live on the eighth floor of a high-rise that had nineteen.

She bought rattan furniture for my room – bed, nightstand, chair, armchair, and some fabric printed in blue from which she sewed curtains, a bedspread, and cushions. The windows looked out on the open sky. A few weeks after moving in, I opened the window in my room and, kneeling on my chair, I began to study the clouds, elbows on the sill.

"Nana! Nana!"

My grandmother was supposedly in heaven.

"Nana! Nana!"

I supposed it would take her some time to appear. I waited a bit.

"Nana!"

Then the intervals between my calls grew shorter.

"Nana! Nana!"

Our bedrooms were separated by a thin wall, you could hear everything.

"Nana! Nana!"

My mother came to see. I was kneeling on the chair.

"Nana!"

My head was raised in the direction of the sky, my back to the door.

"Nana! Nana! Nana!!!"

Then I started to cry.

"Nana Nana Nana Nana Nana Nana Nana Nana Nana Nana Nana Nana Nana ..."

I was out of breath, my shout was transforming, becoming a formless sound.

"Nahnah nahnah nahnah."

A degraded, uninterrupted, badly articulated sound.

"Nananananananananana."

A single vowel, lacking energy.

"Aaaaaaaaaaa … ."

"Christine. Get down from there. Come, come see me. That's the way it is, Christine." I got off the chair and I saw her in the open doorway. "Nana is not going to appear." She came close to me and crouched down to my level. "Come, Christine, come here, don't cry, my little girl."

"You told me she was in the sky. So if she's not in the sky, where is she then, where's Nana?"

"Oh yes, she is in the sky. She can see you. We can't see her. But she does see us."

It was a two-bedroom apartment. Before moving in, we were asked what color wallpaper we preferred for our bedrooms, either blue or yellow, I had chosen blue. It was a wallpaper under-layer in gray-blue. It was neither a turquoise blue, nor a primary blue, nor a sky blue. The yellow, which she had chosen, was a sort of beige.

When I got home from school, I double locked the door and didn't go out again. I walked around the rooms. I went into her bedroom and arranged the objects on her dresser. I put them in the order of their size: vase, ashtray, magazine, pocket mirror. I spread the necklaces into circles.

"Yes, but that's appropriate for a child's taste, Christine."

She put the objects back on a diagonal and the magazines sideways.

"Your seahorse is not in the box, Mama, where is it?"

"It must have been lost in the move."

I had my dolls talk to each other. I talked with them. Or I gathered up burnt matches from the stove and constructed little wooden houses by gluing them onto cardboard.

Sometimes she let me go roller skating on the vinyl flooring tiles in the corridor. There was a glide of about three or four meters between the entry door and the door of the vestibule.

"Mama! Come see!"

She watched me dart out with my palm facing forward, press it on the closed door, launch myself from the half turn, and head off in the other direction.

Then we had dinner, and I went to bed. I looked under the bed to see if anyone was hiding there. She reassured me, returned to the living room.

There was a school in the neighborhood, but I had stayed at Jeanne de France. I took the bus there. The stop was in front of the shopping center, beyond an empty lot. For fear of finding myself shut up in the elevator with boys, I walked up and down the eight floors.

On Saturday, after having made sure while crossing the empty lot that there was light on the eighth floor of the tower, I ran up the stairs and rang the bell.

"Did you forget your keys again!? How scatterbrained you are, my little girl! You are a scatterbrain, you know, Christine."

She put a pot of milk on the fire and took a cake out of the refrigerator. Then she sat down at the corner of the table with me.

She caressed my hair. "Did you have a good day?" She looked at a notebook, a corrected essay, listened to me recite a poem. "That's good, my little fawn." She read my essays, my reports, and my evaluations with her warm hand on mine. "That's good, that's very good, my little fawn."

I caressed the back of her hand. Or, with my fingers, I followed the path of her veins. I turned her hand over and caressed her palm.

"Ooo la la, my little fawn."

She tapped my hand, pushed her chair back to take care of the milk that was rising on the fire, then poured it into my bowl, holding the wooden handle of the little saucepan.

"I'm telling you, you should enter a beauty contest for hands, Mama. You would win. I'm sure of it."

She was laughing.

"Why don't you want to? Why are you laughing?"

Afterwards either we went out, or she watched me walking

around the rooms with lipstick, great wide skirts that belonged to her, and little high heels, making a clacking sound.

"You see, Christine, we can be fine here. You're having fun. We're fine inside. The surroundings, we could care less. Outside isn't great, okay, but outside is outside. We don't live outside."

So as not to say the "ZUP," when people asked for our address, she said Cité Saint Jean.

Just before the urban development zone, there was a little road that went into the country. There were individual houses all along it. Each had its own driveway, paved in stone or covered in gravel, straight or curvy. Each front door was different from the one next to it by the color, the material, a detail, a grating, a handle, or a knocker. She chose her favorite, I had mine, we walked along this little road holding hands, talking about the future and places to live.

"Your hands are soft, Mama."

"Your papa used to tell me that too. He used to say I had a fluid, a potion! He gave me his hand, he'd stay like that for five minutes. And then he'd take it away. He said it was so he could have the pleasure of giving it to me again. He was a little complicated, you know … Then he would give me his hand again."

She took back and then returned her hand to mine, so I would understand.

"They are warm. And so beautiful!"

"You're sweet, my little fawn."

"Why don't you want to enter a beauty contest for hands? You could at least find out about it ..."

"I don't think they exist, you know, Christine."

On Saturdays, I went shopping with her. She'd go into a changing room and I would wait for her on a stool outside. She'd come out, I would look at her, then look at the reflection in the mirror. The saleswoman would say, "That looks good on you, Madame."

We'd smile at each other in the mirror.

"How tall you are!" It was invariable, the salesgirls always said that to her. Back in the changing room, sometimes she would open the curtain and wink at me through the opening.

We went into fabric stores, she would choose the materials and colors for cushions, tablecloths, or couches. The store owner would wrinkle a sample in her hand, then had her touch it. My opinion counted. I would touch it too.

"You are right, Mademoiselle."

As soon as we were back in the street, she would compliment me. I didn't look like her physically, but in matters of taste I necessarily took after her. As for the rest, I had a passion for languages and trips, whereas she couldn't stand train stations.

"One day I'll take you to New York, Mama."

"And your husband, what's he going to say?"

"He can come with us."

"We'll see about that in a few years."

"When I go to America, will you come with me?"

"We haven't got to that yet, eh? We'll see. We'll talk about it later. As it is I don't speak English."

"But I'm going to speak English. When I'm in sixth grade, I'm going to learn English."

"It might be better actually if you made fewer mistakes in your French dictations before thinking about learning English."

"The other day at auntie's, with Marie-Hélène, we were talking about words in the dictionary. I said there are so many that we couldn't understand them all. Just think, Mama, all those words in the dictionary!"

"That's for sure."

"And I asked Marie-Hélène, 'Do you think adults know them all?' You know what she said?"

"No."

"She said, 'Yes, my daddy, he knows them all!' Do you think that's true? Do you think uncle knows all the words in the dictionary?"

"No, he doesn't know them all, and I certainly know more than he does."

"Mama, can I talk to you about something?"

"Of course!"

"You know, sometimes I feel like I'm a little package."

"A little package? What do you mean, a little package?"

"Well, a little package! A little package you carry with you, that you hold by a string."

"Why do you say that?"

"Because."

"But you're not at all a little package. Come on, what makes you think that?"

"When you meet people on the street, when you talk with them, me, I'm just there, I wait."

At Jeanne de France, in my class, I was part of a group of rich girls. They had maids. On their birthdays, sometimes, domestics wearing white gloves served orangeade and scoops of ice cream. Mine was coming. I didn't want to celebrate it because I didn't want them to come to the neighborhood. She convinced me – I could play with my friends in her dressing room. When they came over, we laughed in the dark little room, then paraded around with her skirts and shoes. It went so well that when their mothers came to pick them up, they wanted to stay.

"You see how that went! You don't have to live in a mansion to have a good day after all."

Then they told the whole class what fun they had at my house.

When the seasons changed she would sort her clothes. She stood in front of the mirror in her room wearing a slip and went back and forth between her closet and her mirror, her arms loaded.

She threw the clothes on her bed. She tried them on one by one, the dresses, the sweaters, the skirts, asking herself what was out of style, what didn't fit her anymore, what was still good. Sitting on the armchair in her room, my head resting on the back and my legs stretched out, I gave my opinion: throw it out, give it away, keep it. Until she said: "Okay, that's enough."

"Oh no, Mama, please. Come on, a little longer."

"No, Christine, I'm done now. I've got things to do. We're not going to spend the whole day at it, after all."

"Oh, please!"

I would sit on her lap. I would prop my head against her neck, she enclosed me in her arms. Or, standing, I'd attach myself to her, my arms around her hips. I stayed like that, squeezing her. I added endings to the word "mama." I made it last in my mouth. I played with the pronunciation. I invented words to designate her. She'd roll her eyes and shake her head. I kissed her a lot. Some kisses had names. The one I had baptized "complete kissy" began on her forehead, went down to her eyelids, cheeks, and chin, and ended with kisses on both of her ears.

She often made me laugh until I was out of breath.

I would straddle her knees and she would lower her head, chin on her chest. Once settled, I gave a sharp tap on her shoulders. She raised her head as if I had pressed on an electric switch. And she was a mechanical doll, her automated neck stiff, eyes staring, with a comical expression.

"Again!"

She lowered her head again. I tapped her shoulders again, the stroke had to be quick and sharp. You could hear the sound of the contact. Her expression had to be different each time, and her reaction had to be immediate. That was called "the head."

"Okay, that's enough now, Christine."

I told her everything that happened to me. All the ideas I had. All the thoughts that went through my head. In the evening after dinner, while massaging cream into her hands, sitting in my grandmother's chenille armchair, she talked to me about herself, what she was feeling, her dreams, her projects that would maybe never be done, the images that haunted her.

"You know, Christine, one day I had a dream. I often think about that dream. I am in a tunnel, a very long tunnel, and I'm walking. I'm walking, and I can't see the end of this tunnel. As if it didn't have an end. At some point, I see a tiny light. At the very end of the very end. Very far away. I walk some more. The light grows. But I'm still not getting out of the tunnel. It's so long. I say to myself, 'Oh good god, I'll never get out.' And then all of a sudden, I'm out. And just at that moment, a baby falls into my arms. And I know it's you."

She talked to me while doing other things. Sweeping, ironing. When she ironed, she put on some music. Sometimes, all of a sudden, she would put the iron down. There was a piece she liked, she wanted to dance. She passed in front of me, smiling, turning, spinning. And she moved her hands through the air, her eyes shining. She leaned her head to one side, then to the other.

"You are cheerful, Mama!"

"Do you think?"

"Oh yes! You dance, you sing, you laugh. Oh yes, Mama. You are cheerful."

I was always with her or about to rejoin her. Either I was sitting beside her or I was walking beside her or I was waiting for her. All my pocket change went to the gifts I made for her. I thought about Mother's Day for a long time in advance. The Tranchant jewelry store, on the Avenue de la Gare, was the finest jewelry store in the city. One year I noticed gold earrings enameled in black. From outside you couldn't see the price. The label was turned over. I went in, the saleswoman plunged her hand into the window and gave me a figure. After that, I ran crying to the bus station and took my bus. At the ZUP, I ran across the empty lot. I went up the eight flights in tears and rang the doorbell.

"What's happened to you, Christine?" I was suffocating. "But what is happening? Was there something? Is it something that happened at school?"

I told her.

She took me in her arms. I hooked my fingers behind her neck, and I laid my head on her chest. She caressed my forearms and my wrists.

"It's here, my most beautiful necklace. It's the two arms of my little girl." She caressed my head, my hair, and again my clasped arms. "It's my most beautiful necklace. A more beautiful necklace does not exist."

"Mama …"

"What, my fawn?"

"You know, I … I …"

"What, my little fawn?"

"Mama. I – I would like to tell you something, Mama."

"Yes, my fawn."

"You know, Mama, I love you more, much more, really much, much more, than other girls love their mommies."

One morning early, sounds of crying emerged from my room, she was still in bed. She got up.

I was sobbing in my bed.

"What's the matter, Christine?"

I wasn't answering.

"Come on, now, what's going on?"

I wiped my eyes on the sheet.

"Speak to me! Come on, aren't you going to tell me what's the matter? Christine, come on. Tell me."

"I had a bad dream."

"What did you dream, my little fawn?"

"Well … I dreamed … I was in the bedroom in Rue de l'Indre

… And …" I swallowed my saliva. "I was in my little bed …
beneath the window … And in the big bed there were the other
children of my papa … And …" I fell silent again.

"Try to tell me, my little fawn."

"And my papa … well …"

"Say it."

"He came into the room to say goodbye, but his cheeks … My
papa's cheeks …" The sobbing was twice as loud.

"Calm down. Calm down, Christine. Slowly. Tell me slowly."

"Well …"

"Say it slowly. Be calm."

"Well, my papa, he had … You know … You know those hair-
brushes like the one Marie-Hélène has? With big pokey things.
Okay, well he had one cheek all smooth, and the other cheek …"
It took me a while to continue. "It was covered with pokey things.
Like on the hairbrush."

"Come sit here. Come. Sit in my lap."

"It's not over, my dream …"

"Continue, my little fawn."

"He goes to see his children, he leans in to say goodbye, and
he kisses them with his smooth cheek …" My sobs started up
again. "And then, afterwards … Afterwards, he came over to me.
And for me, Mama … For me, he poked me." I screamed.

"It was a nightmare, my Christine. It's over. It was an ugly
dream. It's over now. Come. Give me a little kiss. It's done, right?

Say it. It's over? It's not reality. You know that, it's a dream. It doesn't exist. That's something that doesn't exist, my little fawn. It's just a bad dream. It's over now. Come so I can give you a little kiss on your little cheek."

I was interested in how many languages my grandfather spoke and the trips he had made. She replied with a certain indifference, then added: "He had a very high opinion of himself, you know. 'We Schwartzes!' I remember he would say that: 'We Schwartzes!'"

One day he came and waited for me when school let out. He took the bus with me. She was surprised to see him when she came home that evening. After dinner he turned to show his profile and told me to take a good look at him. I was supposed to observe the curve that went from the back of his neck to the top of his skull, and notice that it was rounded.

"There are two types of skulls. Brachycephalic and dolichocephalic. Brachycephalic is when the line is straight. Dolichocephalic when it is marked, like mine."

Cupping his hand, he sketched a rounded line in the air and turned to his profile again so I could verify.

"Do you see it? It's less visible with women. Because of the hairdo. But your mother is also dolichocephalic. And you, let me see … Yes. You too."

She said to Nicole later: "He went to get Christine at Jeanne de France … Well, yes, he didn't have our address, when we moved, I didn't tell him where we were going. He gave me such a hard time when I sold the house, claiming I had pocketed everything. I couldn't tell him, after all, that I'd given half to Didi!"

My grandmother had taken her secret to her grave. And she believed it was not up to her to reveal it.

She would tell me about the men she could have married. Charlie, her fiancé when she was sixteen, was kind, attentive. He was always giving her little gifts. Her eyes glazed over as if she was looking at the life she would have had if she had stayed with him. Then she told me about another one.

"Jean Dubois. He was very interesting. He was into a lot of things. He wanted to be a journalist. At his age, he had already traveled a lot. Physically, he was attractive. He was tall. We had style, the two of us, when we danced."

She had met him at a social ball.

"There weren't a lot of guys like him in Châteauroux. And he was a really interesting guy. Not at all ordinary, that Jean Dubois. He stood out with respect to the others."

"Did you already know my papa?"

"Not yet. It was stupid, really, this Jean Dubois, I thought I was too young for me, he was three years younger. That's not a lot, sure. But at the time, that's how it was. You didn't go out with a boy who was younger than you."

"And after my papa, did you know another gentleman?"

"I remained attached to your papa for a very long time. Women were less free than today. It wasn't easy, you know. I had met someone on the beach at Belle-Île, a year or two after you were born, but Nana made it clear that, vis-à-vis the neighbors, that bothered her. 'Think of me,' she said. When you went out with a man, and you weren't married, you know, in those years, you were like a piece of trash."

The Sécurité Sociale managed health insurance and administered hospital establishments financed by employee contributions. Five kilometers from Châteauroux, a psychiatric hospital had just been opened. In Gireugne. It was a revolutionary institution: it broke with the idea of insane asylums. Pretty much everywhere in France, one could still see closed cells, absolute prohibitions about going out, harsh treatments, long-term confinements, uniforms to distinguish the caregivers from the interned, and even, in certain Overseas Departments and Territories, outdoor jet showers to wash the patients standing in line, naked. Gireugne corresponded to the evolution of modern psychiatry, which called into question the notion of normality and dealt with psychosis without isolating those who suffered from it from the rest of humanity. During the previous decades, advances had been achieved that placed talking at the center of care. At Gireugne, there were no bars on the windows, no distinctive clothes, the departments were spread among pavilions at ground level, and the word "crazy" was proscribed. The patients walked freely throughout the establishment, on the paths in the park and at the edges of the forest. They mixed with the staff in the corridors and in the cafeteria, where some drank grape juice in wine glasses to create an illusion and also to maintain the level of sugar in the blood that those who came to be detoxified were used to. This was a few years after the Algerian War. A lot of repatriated people were hired in administrative positions. They lived there with their families in two-story houses of dark brown brick, scattered in the woods and hidden from each other by the foliage of the trees. The pavilions were near the dwellings and grouped around the administration building. The place was called the Psycho-therapeutic Center of Gireugne and was located at the edge of the Poinçonnet Forest.

The job of executive secretary was open. She applied. Her letter was chosen and, after an interview with the director, she was recruited. A car was needed to get there. She went for her license. She absolutely had to get it. I would think about her the day of the driving test. At the exact hour.

She met psychiatrists, psychoanalysts, psychologists. She had conversations with them. Everything depended on early childhood. She did some reading, she learned things. She got along well with the doctor who was the director. Their two offices communicated with each other. She found her work interesting. She had lunch there and told me about her day in the evening.

"There's one patient, Mlle Renaud, who is really very fat, you see, really very very fat, and this Mlle Renaud, she's always dressed in pink, but not a discreet pink, a bright pink, a candy pink. At noon she was walking in the woods, all in pink as usual. And the storeroom person with whom I had lunch today, looking out the window and seeing her walking, said: 'Oh, look at Mlle Renaud, just like a little wild strawberry!!' I laughed. That made me laugh. I admit it. That wasn't nice, was it? But I admit it. I laughed. And you, my fawn, did you have a good day?"

I had got off at my bus stop, as usual, I'd cut across the empty lot, and just when I was getting ready to cross the street: "On the other sidewalk there were two girls my age, you see, who were arguing. And one of them asked the other: 'So where is your father?' and the other answered: 'I don't have one.'"

We were sitting at the corner of the table in the kitchen. She finished her mouthful, put down her fork and knife, and turned toward me: "However, that little girl has a father. Everybody has one. You know it, Christine. We already talked about it. Maybe her mother didn't tell her. But she has one. Everybody has one. She maybe doesn't know him, but she has one. Me too, I have one. I didn't live with him very much. But he's my father. I have one. You too, you have one. Auntie also has one. Everybody.

And you. You don't know him. Or rather, you don't remember him. You've seen him. You don't remember him but you've seen him. You saw him the first time when you were two, during a vacation. The second time, you were three. You saw him a third time, you were six. You never saw him for long, it's true. And he came to see you when you were a baby. You were in your cradle, you don't remember. That little girl also has a father. Even if she's never seen him. Everybody has one."

The chief accountant came from Algiers. His family lived in one of the little houses of dark brown brick, and he had a daughter my age. She dropped me off at their house on Wednesday mornings and picked me up in the afternoon. One evening we didn't go straight home. She took me to a little office where a psychologist asked me some questions.

It was already dark out.

"Would you please draw me a family, Christine?"

When I left the office, she went in, I waited for her in the corridor. Then we got in the car.

"Good. She says everything's fine. She asked you to draw a family, I think …"

"Yes."

"She says everything's fine, okay. She showed me your drawing. You can see things from children's drawings. And you, very good. You drew the father. So that's very good."

"Well sure, I was supposed to draw a family!"

"Yes, and that's very good, Christine. You did the father really well. Then you made a little girl, that's good. And then you did the mother. You drew a balanced family. That's really good."

She turned toward me, smiling: "The father – you made him very small. He's a really little fellow, but he's there. That's very good. He's very little, in a corner of your page, but he exists. You made a little girl who is about the same size as the father. But that's good. Because everybody's there, everybody's in their place. And you made a mother. The mother ... the mother, you made a mother, now that ... A mother ... Enormous! Taking up the whole page."

She threw her head back. She laughed openly.

Big concrete pillars supported the nineteen floors of the building. That made a large peristyle around the entryway. To enter the building, we had to go under these columns. Drafts blew in there. She parked the car, we went into the peristyle, she walked fast, her head down, shoulders drawn in.

"Oh drat, these drafts! They're something else!!"

Our hair went flying back because of the gusts, our skirts were glued to our thighs. It was hard to go forward. The only thing about this ZUP that she allowed herself to criticize was the circulation of the wind between these pillars.

The year I was twelve, the school organized a trip to Venice. On our return, she came to fetch me at the station, under a heavy gray sky. We talked in the car as we passed by the cement façades on the Boulevard de Bruyas.

"You cannot imagine how beautiful it was, Mama! Venice is beautiful! It's beautiful. You cannot imagine. I know it cost a lot, but it was really worth it. It was extraordinary."

"The whole class going and you staying here!? Huh? No way!"

"If I go back, will you come with me?"

"We'll see. As it is, I don't speak Italian."

"But all the shopkeepers there speak French. And it's beautiful. We were in our t-shirts. There was magnificent sunshine. Whereas here, look how ugly it is."

"Of course if you compare it with Châteauroux …"

"At any rate, I'm not staying here. I'm going to leave."

"Oh, you know, you say that, you may never do it!"

"Oh yes, I'll be leaving. You'll see."

"That's it. I'll see."

The following year she got a call from Mme Borgeais, a friend of hers who worked at the Caisse. "Quick, quick, Rachel, I have to tell you something. Okay, I'll tell you. Quickly. Very quickly. I'll tell you quickly. The girl's father just called the Caisse. And he asked for you. We told him you don't work here anymore. That you're at Gireugne. He's going to call you. He said he'd be calling you right away. That's why I'm calling, before."

It was in the middle of the afternoon. They hung up. A few minutes later, her extension rang.

"Hello, Rachel, it's Pierre. How are you?" My father's voice was clear and poised.

"Quite well. And you? How are you?" Hers too.

"I'm calling because I have something to tell you, Rachel. I'm probably going to leave Strasbourg and come closer to you." His father had just retired. Michelin was offering him the position of Director. "We can see each other more easily, Paris–Châteauroux isn't far."

"Yes. That would be good."

"But how are you, Rachel? I … I mean, you … I mean, how are you?"

"Fine. I'm really fine."

"The hospital isn't too tough?"

"Not at all, it's going very well."

"How long has it been, that you've been in this hospital, I didn't know …"

"I'm not confined, Pierre. I work here. I am in charge of the staff and I'm secretary to the director."

"Oh very good. Forgive me. I hadn't understood."

That was the first time she'd heard his voice again since the morning when she'd said, "Now you leave," and he had disappeared down the lane.

Five years had passed. His crossing the courtyard, my saying goodbye and calling him Papa, watching him go from the top of the stairs, like a child at a play, her shutting the door, starting to weep. Since that time, she was no longer angry.

She had almost stopped thinking about him. Her work had evolved, she had regained confidence in herself. But on the emotional level, she'd had only unambiguous encounters, with married men or people she didn't like.

"The guys here are all short, I'd really like to meet someone taller than five foot five."

She bought a magazine, *The French Hunter*, which specialized in hunting, fishing, and DIY, and published personal ads.

"I'm very happy being a mother. But I'm not only a mother. I also have a woman's life. I have to live my woman's life. I'm very lucky to have you, but you are a little girl, you see. You are my little girl. It's not the same. I would really like to meet a man my age. Do you understand?"

"Why isn't it the same? Because I'm a child?"

"It's not the same kind of love. It's difficult to explain. I need to have the life of a woman. A woman needs to be loved by a man."

"So you think you aren't having a woman's life?"

"No, of course, I do have a woman's life. But not completely. I'm alone as an adult, in my life. To live my life. Make decisions. Go on vacation, share things with someone my own age. You realize that all the people we know, besides Nicole, live as couples. Grownups need other grownups, to talk to. Do you understand?"

"But we talk, don't we?"

"That's true, Christine. And you are the biggest joy of my life. I don't know how I would manage if you weren't here …"

"I love you, Mama."

"Me too, my little fawn. Lots and lots. But it's not the same love. Do you understand?"

"What's the one that's strongest?"

"There isn't a strongest one. They aren't the same sort of thing. Each one is just as strong as the other. But they are different. They aren't similar. Do you understand?"

"No. Not very well. I don't see what the difference is."

"Let's see. How am I going to explain it to you? Love for your child is a very very great love. Immense. Certainly the biggest, if really you have to say which one is the biggest. But it's not the same kind of thing."

"So what are the differences?"

"Do you remember Victor Hugo's poem? 'O, a mother's love, love none can forget . . . Each has a share, and each one's share is all'? Good. So that is the love between a mother and her child. It never dies. It never comes to an end. It's an eternal love. Love between a man and a woman is something else again. It can happen that it's not eternal. But it is also very strong."

"Why didn't you get married with my papa?"

"Because he didn't want to, I suppose. He wasn't settled as far as his professional future was concerned. And he wanted to stay free. There were several reasons that got combined …"

"How come you wanted to have a child?"

"Because it was a great love, Christine."

"How come you didn't get married, then?"

"He had specific ideas about the type of wife he wanted, I think I didn't correspond to what he was looking for. He wanted a more docile wife, I think. And then … It's hard, you know. No doubt that wasn't all there was to it."

"What else was there?"

"Well, particularly on the social level."

"What's that?"

"My family, my background, my situation, Nana, all of that … for him it wasn't … It wasn't what he was looking for."

"He didn't like Nana?"

"He hardly knew her. It's not that he didn't like Nana. But among my relatives there wasn't any wealth. You understand? He came from a certain milieu. He wanted someone he could introduce to his family, who could increase his status on that level. You know, when I was pregnant, I wrote him. And his mother happened upon the letter. And she said to him, 'Look out. She wants to get hold of a wealthy young man.' All I wanted, according to her, was that. They were people like that, you see."

"Yes … But there's something I don't understand. He wanted a child with you anyway?!"

"We both wanted you, Christine. Because we loved each other. He too. Believe me. We loved each other a lot, your papa and I. Lots and lots. He told me he wouldn't look after you, but he wanted us to have a child together."

"And you accepted that, you wanted it all the same?! Even though he said he wouldn't look after me?"

"Yes. Because …" She got a lump in her throat. "Because I never loved anyone as much as I loved your papa." For a moment she had a faraway look in her eyes. "And then, I said to myself he could change his mind … It's a lucky thing I said that to myself, actually. Otherwise you wouldn't be here, maybe. Hmm, my little fawn? That would be a real shame! Huh? My Christine. Don't you think?"

"He loved you a lot, too, Mama?"

"Yes. A lot."

In June, like every year, as soon as it turned sunny, we went to Bellebouche. The adults chose a spot near the water and spread a blanket out. Then the children were permitted to go swimming. While I was putting my bathing suit on, the youngest of my cousins pointed a finger at me:

"Hhhaaa!!!!!! Christine has hairs on her bottom!!!"

My mother had explained to me that I was going to become

an adolescent. It would be a transformation. And the proof that I was growing up. I was going to have what they call periods. Each month I would have a little blood flow.

In the end, my father didn't take the job at Michelin. The salary they were offering was not comparable to what he had at the European Council. He wasn't going to move closer to us. But the phone call alone had changed things. A new phase began.

The epistolary rhythm started up again. He would call her from time to time at Gireugne. We didn't have telephone service. And in any case he preferred to call from the Council during business hours, rather than from home. They told each other their news. He lived near the Orangerie in Strasbourg, with his wife and their little boy, François, the name they had agreed on for me before my birth, if I had not been a girl.

Rachel and Christine Schwartz
Block 9, Apt. 262
Rue Michelet
Châteauroux

My dear, dear Rachel,
All sorts of problems have come to spoil my optimism of last year. The most serious was the formal notice that we have to move out of our apartment – the owner wants to sell it. The outcome of this matter

remains unresolved. You can imagine the tension one feels when looking for a new dwelling, precipitously, all the while hoping not to have to move. As a result I have perhaps seemed quite distant.

Nevertheless, I have been thinking a lot about you two. I actually telephoned you in mid-March but didn't reach you. According to the answer they gave me at your office, Christine was sick and that kept you home. Therefore her nice letter telling me afterwards about her health problems for the semester did not come as a surprise. On the contrary, it reassured me, because now I know she is fine.

My love to you both. I kiss your hands.

Pierre

There was another letter in the envelope.

My dear little Christine,

What a pretty card you sent me! And also, you are quite right to regret the time lost during the second semester because of your illness. But that's not too serious, because you realize, all on your own, that it's a bother to lose months of work. I am sure you will make up your work and you'll be the head of the class again.

That's what I wish for you, and also for solid good health now.

I give you a kiss and thank you again with all my heart for your nice letter.

Papa

Soon after, his phone calls became less frequent. His letters again became few and far between. He was preoccupied. His father had Alzheimer's. This man, whom he had admired so much, would read the same edition of *Le Monde* all day long, didn't recognize him anymore, had become incontinent; the words he spoke were incoherent, the nurses treated him like a child. My father couldn't stand this decline.

Then she received a letter informing her of the man's death.

He called her a few weeks later. Proposing that she meet him in Paris.

Upon her return she handed me a package.

"Here, Christine, it's from your father. There wasn't any gift-wrap." It was soft to the touch. "Open it!"

The bag contained a colored plastic pouch, it was a globe you had to blow up. And there was a half-circle in rigid plastic on which the meridians were marked. You hung the valves of the globe on it. You could make it turn. The whole thing was light and unstable.

"Okay, I have to show you something. I promised him. He really insisted on it. He said, 'Show her where Brazil is.' So I'll show you."

We turned the globe, she put her finger on a broad expanse in mauve.

"There. It's there."

"Why Brazil?"

"Because it's big, I suppose. He said to me, 'You'll show her Brazil, it's a big country.' That's all he said."

"And you didn't ask him why? Russia is even bigger!"

"Listen, I'm just telling you what he said, he didn't say anything else. Just write him if you want to know exactly why, me, I don't know. He said to me, 'You'll show her Brazil, won't you, it's a big country.' He really insisted."

Dear little Christine,

It was impossible for me to answer sooner because I wasn't here during the holidays. Your letter is really sweet. Now I can picture you poring over your books and notebooks or listening to your teacher in class. Your grades are magnificent and I find it even more wonderful that you are interested in so many things.

To learn things is one of the greatest joys in life, and I marvel that you have understood that so well.

If you feel like it, I would like to receive another letter from you in which you tell me what you do in class or what games you like to play. And I will tell you what I like. That way we will know each other when we are able to see each other. . .

Why Brazil? Maybe because it's a country whose wealth is all in the future, like you for whom the globe was intended.

Give a great big kiss to your mom for me, and here's a big kiss for you.

Your papa

The city of Châteauroux was larger at that time than it was later on. There were still factories and some pretty stores in the streets of the center of town. But there wasn't much to it. She found it stifling. It was a recurring topic of conversation between her and Nicole. Could they meet men they liked here? Where? At the movies? The man in the next seat? Who? Could things take a turn for the better if they stayed here? Nicole had tried to leave. A position had opened up at the state health insurance office in a little city near Annecy, a region she liked, she had applied for the job. She had felt lonely there, she came back. She considered this return a failure. She felt like she had missed her chance.

"Okay, Christine, I have to talk to you. Come here. Sit down. Okay. Here's the thing. We have the possibility of leaving Châteauroux. There is a position at the Sécurité Sociale in Reims, it was announced in the notices of employee transfers. And I applied for the job. It's at the health insurance office. That's less interesting than what I'm doing at Gireugne. And if they take me, I'll have a reduction in salary at first. But it would allow us to leave Châteauroux. Afterwards we can see how things might evolve. In any case, it's not going to happen right away. There's a whole procedure, it's quite long. I won't know if my candidacy has been retained until the end of the summer. People from all over France are going to apply. There will be an exam. If they take me, we'll see. I can always refuse. And if we leave, I'll have six months to take back my job in Châteauroux if things don't work out. Like Nicole did. Reims is in the East. It's in Champagne, the region of champagne."

"Do you mean in the East, next to Germany?"

"No, it's closer to Paris. It's a university city. Later on that will be good for you. Physically, they're easterners. It's not at all like here, it's not the same style. They are taller, for one thing. They are a little reserved, but sincere, apparently. It's not superficial. It's not like in the south, for example, you see? What would you think about it?"

"It's bigger than Châteauroux?"

"A lot bigger. It's a much richer city. There are cinemas. There are theaters. There's a Cultural Center. It's not like here, Avenue de la Gare and Rue Victor Hugo. And it's a very pretty city. There is no forest, but there are vineyards. Apparently it's really beautiful, the landscape. There is a very beautiful cathedral. And if you get to know your papa one day, it's closer to Strasbourg. A lot closer."

"How many kilometers away?"

"Oh … I'd say four hundred … Besides, we'll have to have a discussion about that. It could be a chance for you, on the legal level. From a judicial point of view. There is a new law about filiation that's just been passed. The procedure for recognition of illegitimate children has been simplified. I have to check with him, but if your papa agrees, all he has to do is go to a lawyer to change the will, and then to the Châteauroux city hall. That's all.

And then you would use your father's name. Like all children. There wouldn't be 'father unknown' written on your official documents. You also would have to agree, of course. You would have a new name. It's a big change."

"I wouldn't be Christine Schwartz anymore?"

"No. You would have your papa's name."

"Christine Angot?"

"Yes. So therefore, you're the one this concerns first of all. What do you think? Would you like to get to know your papa? And use his name? If we go to Reims, we can get it done discreetly. The job starts in January. If we get this done before the end of the year, we can sign you up for school with your new name. Hmm? Would you like to?"

"Yes."

"That way you'd be using your papa's name, you'd be legally recognized as his daughter. Just like his legitimate children. There wouldn't be any difference. If we go to Reims, we wouldn't need to tell the story of our lives to everybody. No one would ask you any questions, since you would be in a different school ... What do you think?"

"Yes."

"You'd like to get to know your papa?"

"Yes."

"And you'd be happy about changing your name?"

"It would be fun, I'd be in the A's. At school, when they call the roll, I'll be the first. Whereas now it's Marie-Osmonde Balsan, and I'm the last. It would be fun. And it's easier to spell. My girl-friends think he's dead. Over there I'd be able to talk about him."

"We could go to Strasbourg this summer. We'd go via Reims. You would start in the fall in eighth grade at Châteauroux. And if I get the job, we would leave after Christmas. That would make you change schools in the middle of the year, it's not ideal but … Well, it can't be perfect on every point."

During the summer vacation, we planned to go to the east of France. We would tour. We would visit Reims. We would stop off in Toul, one of her girlfriends had just settled there because she was in love with a man from Lorraine who ran a bar. Then we would go to Strasbourg. I would get to meet my father. After that we would spend a week of vacation at Gérardmer. Maybe he would join us there.

Her friends in Toul left us their apartment. They slept above their bar. The neighborhood was not in the center of town, but the apartment was gleaming. One morning:

"Look, Mama, my underpants, they're all soiled." I was showing her the crotch.

"No, Christine … It's not soiled, it's not dirty."

"Yes it is, look, it's all black."

"That's not what you think. It's not dirty. No."

"So what is it, then?"

"Well, it's …"

"Oh no!!"

"Yes, my little fawn."

"I don't want it to be that. It's out of the question."

"But that's what it is."

"No. No no. No."

"Yes, my little fawn, that's what it is."

I burst into tears.

"For goodness sake, it means you are a big girl. There is no reason to cry."

"Are you sure it's that? Maybe it's something else …"

"No, Christine, that's what it is. You are thirteen, it's perfectly normal. We'll go buy some tampons at the drug store, it's really easy to put them in, you won't even realize you have anything. You won't think about it anymore."

I didn't manage to insert the tampon myself. I called her, I lay down on my back, with my legs in the air, spread wide apart so she would have the necessary visibility.

My father telephoned. He had reserved two rooms for us in Strasbourg, she wrote down the address of the hotel. They agreed on a day and time. Then she handed me the phone.

I was hearing his voice for the first time. Tears came to my eyes. I couldn't speak. I handed the phone back to her. They said a few words to each other, and she hung up.

The meeting took place in one of the two reserved rooms. The wallpaper was yellow and the room was full of sunlight.

There was a knock.

"Yes. Come in …"

I threw myself into his arms, pressing myself against him. I cried for a few minutes, huddled against him like that. Then we went out.

His car was parked in front of the hotel, it was a light blue Citroen DS. He held the front door for her until she was settled in her seat, opened the back door for me, walked around the car and got behind the wheel. He was driving us to the café at the station, which had Alsatian specialties. When we arrived, he pointed us to a booth.

It was very hot. He explained the climate to us. Winds blew from the Atlantic. They were blocked by the Vosges Mountains. They did not blow over the plains in Alsace. Strasbourg had a continental climate. It was hot in the summer, cold in winter. The farther one went toward Eastern Europe, the greater the difference in the climate. We were given menus. Lifting his eyes from his menu, he explained to us what *waterzoï* and *spätzle* were, and the different types of sauerkraut. Then he called a waiter. My mother ordered her meal with a false assurance. Her voice went from loud to inaudible. And a question mark seemed to hover over everything she was saying.

My father had to return to the Council. At the end of the meal, he smoked a cigarillo and took us back to the hotel.

"So, it went well! Are you happy?"

"He's wonderful, Mama. I didn't think I had such an extraordinary papa."

"I didn't go get you just any old person, did I!"

"Oh no, really! It's the first time in my life I've spoken to someone as intelligent! And as interesting! If I had been living with him, do you realize all the things I would have learned? And everything I would know now … But one thing is bothering me, I can't seem to call him Papa. Do you think I could call him Pierre?"

"Probably. You could ask him."

"Did you hear him when I asked him to speak German? Did you hear his accent? And in English? How beautiful was that?! Do you realize that in Germany they take him for a German. And it's like that in several countries! It's brilliant. It's brilliant to be so intelligent. And so cultivated. I would really like to take after him."

"You know, maybe I don't speak any foreign languages, but I'm not stupid either."

"I know, but his intelligence exceeds the norm."

"For heaven's sake, what a thing to say! Do you think he would have been interested in me if I had been stupid?"

"We have the same hands, you never told me. Did you notice or weren't you paying attention?"

"Maybe, yes."

I put my hands right in front of her eyes. "Look at my thumb. The shape of my thumb is the same as his. Exactly. Look. Look at my fingers. Do you see it? You never noticed? Don't you think I look like him? We have the same hair. It's kind of bizarre. And we have exactly the same tastes. Yet we've never lived together. It's funny. It's incredible."

In the evening he took us to a restaurant on the second floor of a half-timbered building.

"It's the best Italian in Strasbourg. If you like pizza you should have one, they are famous. Or you might have an osso bucco or spaghetti all'arrabbiata. Do you like Italian cuisine? What do you like?"

He pronounced "arrabbiata" two times, once in the French manner, once in the Italian, rolling the r's at the back of his throat. He ordered an osso bucco, and she had veal scallops. We talked about the pleasure that eating out in a restaurant represents.

"It's enjoyable, but it remains expensive. There are people who cannot afford it. And when you go to a cheap restaurant, it's not at all the same …"

"Well I, Rachel, do not share your opinion!"

"Meaning?"

"Judgments are relative. A person who frequents fine restaurants finds pleasure in places that are nicer than the ones he is used to. Agreed?"

"Yes."

"A person who has never been to a gourmet restaurant ... would not make comparisons with a gourmet restaurant. That goes without saying. Rather, with a restaurant he knows. And if he's in a more elegant place, he will have an excellent evening. Certainly even, that's what's ... okay ... certainly even a better evening than a person dining in a restaurant of a much superior level but one that's ordinary from his point of view, conforming to his habits. Whereas the other one will be very happy in what you're calling a cheap restaurant."

"Oh, you think so?"

"For sure, Rachel. And it's basically a good thing, isn't it?"

"Hmm ..."

"In certain restaurants, ones that are a bit chic and maybe a little too stuffy besides, a lot of people do not feel at ease, you know."

"Yes. Maybe."

"Whereas others feel at home. And are perfectly relaxed."

"Maybe. I don't know. I'm not sure I really understand. Perhaps you are right."

"And what about you, Christine, give us your opinion."

"Anyway, it's delicious. It's really good, this pizza. I've never eaten such a good pizza."

He laughed.

We got back into his luxury Citroen. He parked, walked with us into the entryway. Then in the elevator. They said goodnight to me in front of the door to my room. They continued down the corridor. They made love. He didn't want to get home too late. He left around midnight.

We went to Gérardmer.

He joined us at the end of the week. He arrived in the morning. We had lunch. The three of us went for a walk along the lake. He headed out at nightfall.

She was happy to have seen him. Sad to see him leave. Every time it was arrival–departure. Nothing was stable. We were standing behind the car as it drove off, and she was silently crying. I put my hand out to her. And I squeezed her wrist.

Just before leaving, he came to see me in my room. The next day, when he telephoned, he asked the front desk to connect him directly with her.

We returned to Châteauroux at the end of the summer. A few days later, the reply from Reims arrived. She was still in the running. The exam was to take place during the fall.

At the beginning of October she received a card from London. It was an aerial view, you could see the Parliament Building, Big Ben, and Westminster Abbey.

On assignment in London for a few days, I note that the climate here is magnificent! At least during these last days of September. Be well!

Pierre

A longer letter arrived two weeks later.

Dear Rachel,

You proposed that we maintain a correspondence. This proposal pleased me. Unfortunately, as you see, I have little time for writing. That does not mean I am not thinking about you, about both of you, you know it. I would so like you both to be happy. Tell me about what you are doing or plan to do, your Sunday outings, everything. You mustn't wait for my letters to write. You are so reserved that I am obliged to insist. Write to me! Not as if you were reporting things seriously, stiffly sitting on a bench. But as if you let your hand rest in mine. You know I listen to you much better that way. Actually, your last letter was a bit like an offered hand. I am taking hold of it. I am keeping it in my hands and listening.

It often happens that I subject the calendar to all sorts of manipulations to see if I can find some free time so I can visit you. It's really difficult. And then, it is also necessary to lay the groundwork. I would like to know if you, if both of you, would like me to visit. I scarcely dare ask this question because it already seems a bit like a commitment. But I do need to know where you are with this. Don't *forget it's been a long time since I received a letter from you or from Christine. And, in such cases, one always tends to make alarming hypotheses.*

My fingers wrapped in your fingers,
Pierre

Everything came together in the month of November. The written test took place at the beginning of the month and after that everything went very fast.

The following week, she was called in for the oral. She was running through the streets, her train left at nine, she was late. She arrived at the station out of breath. The train was at the platform. She ran through the underground tunnel, up the stairs, the last meters. But the doors of the car closed in front of her. All her hopes collapsed. She went back through the tunnel. In the concourse was Jean Dubois, her suitor when she was twenty. He had missed his train too. He was pacing back and forth. They hadn't seen each other for years.

"If you like, Rachel, I have a car, we could try to catch it at Vierzon."

When they arrived at Vierzon, they decided to continue.

"Rachel, do you remember where we met?"

"Of course. At a dance at the Hôtel du Faisan!"

"Yes, it was a Saturday. You were with friends. The following Monday we ran into each other in the city, do you remember?"

"Of course, Jean, I remember it very well, it was around noon, I was going home for lunch. I was about to take the Grande Echelle and who do I see in the street all of sudden, saying *Hello, Rachel*?"

"It's okay for me to say it now, I had looked up where you lived and arranged it so I would be on your route at lunchtime. When you saw me, I had been waiting for you. I had been walking up and down the neighborhood for half an hour."

They separated at Porte d'Orléans. They were in a hurry, they didn't exchange addresses. She took the metro and got to the train station at Gare de l'Est.

The director of the Caisse de Reims had a touch of a southwestern accent and very black hair combed toward the back.

"You will be informed very soon, Madame Schwartz. And if you are hired, an apartment will be held for you on the first of January, through the COPLORR."

That was an agency to which the Caisse contributed the employer's one percent for lodging; it could grant an apartment to the organization on an emergency basis, to house an employee.

The next day she received a call at Gireugne. She had passed, in first place.

Things sped up. She handed in her notice at the ZUP. And she wrote to my father, apologizing for the long time that had passed since her last letter. She had been preoccupied with her application. They hired her. We were going to move. Would he agree to recognize me before the end of the year so she could enroll me in my new school with my new name?

He agreed.

The attestation of inheritance was modified by his lawyer in Strasbourg. Who advised him to think it over carefully. At any rate, this modification would not be in effect until after the change in my civil status. That change had to be done at the Châteauroux city hall. He was supposed to show up in person. A visit was planned for the end of November.

He arrived at the ZUP one evening, having driven all afternoon. He had a headache. He was very tired. He was subject to these headaches. It was the first time he set foot in the city since the morning when she shooed him out of Rue de l'Indre.

She showed him around the apartment. When I was in bed, they sat in the living room.

"I am not going to recognize Christine, I'm really sorry, Rachel. I am very happy to see you, and we will see each other whenever it is possible to. But I'm not going to recognize her, it's a bad idea, I assure you. I have thought it over carefully."

"What? But that's why you came! Are you telling me now that you've changed your mind?"

"The situation has been the way it is for thirteen years. Unlike you, not everyone considers this law advantageous. This type of progress can even cause a lot of harm. Some people say …"

"Who?"

"You're not the only one in the world, Rachel, this change may be convenient for you, but within my family it would be a source of difficulties. Things are not as easy as you imagine." He glanced around the apartment. "You don't need me."

"But why … But what does … ?"

"Christine has no connection with the rest of my family. I am not going to impose her on my in-laws. There is no reason to. They are very nice people. I don't have to subject them to a situation that does not concern them; besides, they know nothing about it."

"But after all, Pierre, you had agreed, you know!"

"I thought about it. Don't you ever think about things?"

"Yes I do, that's just it. Do you think it's right that Christine should start life with 'father unknown' as her civil status? She'll have to live with that all her life. Whereas you have the possibility of recognizing her. You're here, you came for that. Because you are her father. Why are you backing off?"

"I'm distrustful."

"What is it you distrust? Whom do you distrust?"

"You have always wanted to become part of my family, haven't you?"

"Excuse me?"

"That's not what I meant to say …"

"Right now this is about Christine. She's the one who needs

to be accepted by her father as his daughter. As for me, I understood a long time ago."

They argued for a good part of the night. The next day they went to the Châteauroux City Hall and the line "father unknown" disappeared from my birth certificate.

On December 31, we had dinner at the home of my uncle's parents. The conversation was about the future resettlement, the period of adaptation, the discouragement we shouldn't give in to. My uncle, my aunt, and my cousins were there. At the moment we separated, we cried, the goodbyes continued in the corridor, then on the sidewalk.

We slept in a room upstairs, and we left the following morning. My uncle's mother was crying in front of the door of her house. We waved. We waved for one last time. She bent down to see us, framing her face in the window. The car began to move. A road map was spread open in my lap. It was cold. I had a little red hat pulled down over my forehead. The highway was deserted. The poplar trees paraded past, Déols, Levroux, Bourges, Issoudun, Auxerre, Tonnerre, Épernay. Towards the end of the drive, we began to see the hillsides planted with vines, the stocks were low and denuded by winter.

❧

The apartment was located in Châtillons, an area in the southern periphery of Reims near the village of Cormontreuil, in the midst of a group of low-income apartments built two or three years earlier. The actual low-income units were grouped in the center of the project. Further out, scattered in little pockets, were short, chunky, somewhat massive towers recognizable by their façades of more or less bronze-colored tiles. Eight floors high, they housed apartments where the rent was higher, and people who earned more than the maximum income were allowed to rent them. These were better kept than the rest of the project, they were surrounded by lawns, the mailboxes were made of dark wood and the doorknobs were steel. A two-bedroom apartment had been allocated to us on the sixth floor of one of the towers. When we arrived, the impression was not negative.

Dear Rachel,

I was pleased to learn from Christine the address of the apartment you have found. I am eager to come see you. Christine must have told you that I think I will be able to take a few days' vacation during the week of February 25. It would give me great joy to spend a few days with you, if it is not inconvenient for you. My last stay in Châteauroux has left me with beautiful memories, I owe them to Christine, whom it is wonderful to get to know, and to you as well. You were able to make your case so well, with all your intelligence and your sensitivity, which are great, and you were so kind to me.

*From time to time I regret an answer I gave you because I thought it
was true, an answer that may have made you feel hurt. I regret it,
because it may have made you feel hurt, and also because it is perhaps
not true. Be happy. I kiss your hands. Write to me.*

Pierre

Will Christine be on vacation the week of February 25?

She didn't ask herself whether she was happy or unhappy at
Châtillons. Her preoccupations were to reimburse a bank loan
and to settle into her job. She was responsible for the personnel.
The four employees of the department, one of whom had been a
candidate for the position she held, were waging war against her.
Every day there were disagreements, refusals to do what she
asked, arrivals without a good morning, departures without a
goodbye, unpleasant comments and once, even, in a corridor, a
remark about her Jewishness addressed to no one in particular:
"Rachel Schwartz, isn't that a Jewish name?"

Nicole had warned her, she shouldn't get discouraged. And
for the first six months she would have to struggle with the desire
to go back.

Dear Rachel,

*Your work training in Nancy, if it is confirmed, will complicate
our plans, it takes place precisely during the week when I am free. I
took vacation days on purpose to come see you. I can be in Reims on*

Wednesday, February 27, and stay some time, the 28th, the 1st, maybe the 2nd, I could leave on the 3rd. It is essential for me to learn your plans as quickly as possible. If your training is confirmed, would you prefer that I meet you in Nancy? I am eager for the 27th to arrive.

I hope you will adapt quickly to your new situation, without too much trouble. I am sure you will succeed and will return to a comfortable life before long. I am sure of it because success depends less on circumstances than on people, and as a result you will succeed. I am impatient to hear from you about the details of your settling in and your first days in your new employment. Do know that I am thinking of you.

Pierre

For my fourteenth birthday, I received a package that came from Châteauroux. My girlfriends sent me a silver napkin ring with a stylized C, which came from the Tranchant jewelry store, and a book about adolescence, *Virginia is Fourteen*.

At the end of February, my father came and waited for me when school let out. I had a new friend, Véronique. I told her: "I'm not waiting for you. My father is coming to get me, I'm off. See you Monday!"

He was smoking, leaning with his elbow on the open window of his car, a light blue Peugeot 604, he had changed cars. We went to Châtillons. I gave him a tour of the apartment. My mother returned home a few hours later.

"Mama, Mama. Come, come. Come. Come, I'm going to give you a complete kissy."

She let herself fall to the couch, I grabbed hold of her, and while I was kissing her according to the rules of the complete kissy, he was reading *Le Monde* sitting near the sliding door. At that hour, a little natural light still reached the pages, spread wide on the round skirted table. His armchair had its back to the balcony and was near the couch. Nothing was far. The room was not big. While I was kissing my mother's forehead, eyelids, cheeks, nose, chin, and ears, she caught a glance coming from him. He raised his eyes above the newspaper. It was fleeting. It lasted only an instant. But she had the impression his gaze contained something unpleasant. She couldn't have said what, it was an impression. It could have been a projection on her part. She swept it away.

He put his paper down and got up. "Did you have a good day?"

The best restaurants in the region were outside the city, but the Continental, at the corner of Erlon Square and the Esplanade, was in his guide and seemed pleasant. After going up a dozen steps, we arrived in a large circular room, entirely glassed in, which overlooked the square. He sat with his back to the windows, and we opposite him. Behind him we could see the leaves on the trees.

I had pink crevettes for an appetizer, and then smoked salmon.

They had oysters. Then he had a Chateaubriand steak with béarnaise sauce and she had a sirloin steak. The meat came with narrow, beautifully grilled French fries.

"Oh, this meat is so good, Pierre!"

He cut a piece and put it in his mouth.

"Hummm."

He closed his eyes, the better to evaluate it.

"It's good, isn't it, eh, Pierre?"

"Humm … Oh yes. It's rare, a good piece of meat. Humm … Like this one. Nice and tender. Humm!"

"A good rib steak is delicious. It's very good here, the meat. You brought us to an excellent place, Pierre. It's a little copious, but it's really very good."

"As for me, what I miss in Alsace is seafood. I never eat oysters in Strasbourg, you know!"

"But you love them so much!"

"Yes, but the freshness of the oysters one finds over there is nothing like the ones you can get in Paris, or even here, it's too far from the fishing ports. In Germany I never have fish either."

He asked us questions about our settling in, our isolation from the city, her difficulties at the office, the studies I was planning on pursuing, my school. We ordered dessert. The specialty of the house was profiteroles. Seeing them coming we gave a cry. Then we returned to Châtillons. She put some sheets on the divan in the living room.

The following morning they hadn't been unfolded. He was in the kitchen having breakfast.

She was coming out of the bathroom.

"What's going on, Christine? Is something wrong? What's happening?"

I was crying.

"Christine, tell me. What's happening? What's wrong?"

"Nothing."

"Oh come on, tell me."

"Nothing, Mama. I promise. It's just that it feels weird to see that you slept in the same room. Since you put sheets on the divan yesterday … I didn't think …"

"Does that bother you?"

"No."

"Are you sure?"

"Yes."

"So why are you crying? Are you sure it doesn't bother you?"

"Yes, yes. It's normal. It doesn't bother me. It's normal for a papa and a mama to sleep together. It's just that I'm not used to it."

She went off to work.

A few weeks later a large envelope mailed in Strasbourg arrived. It contained a copy of the notarized act by which I figured on the succession. There was the complete civil status of my father with the date of his marriage. That date was six months later than the visit in Châteauroux that had ended with "now you leave." The one that had made her cry so much the time he told her he was married. In fact he was lying.

Dear Rachel,

I am saddened by the news you tell me about your psychological state. I would have thought you would more easily overcome the difficulty of starting out. Have you asked for and obtained a meeting with your director, as I advised you to do? In any case, your decision to remain in Reims seems to me a good one, at first sight.

It will not come as a consolation to you to learn that I am having problems, but perhaps it will be a good reason to give yours less importance. Following some digestive problems, I consulted a doctor, who diagnosed a gall bladder atonia and prescribed a dietary regime (not too rigorous). I don't think it's too serious. But I won't be fully reassured until I know the results of the analyses that I am going to have to undergo. I am therefore waiting for the end of the month of April with a feeling of uncertainty, which is always unpleasant.

As for the little lies, dear Rachel, you have to count them for nothing beside the big fat truths. Sometimes they come into the conversation in the form of formulas of politeness, and you mustn't grant them any more importance. Don't you commit some yourself, say, by omission, for example?

I think about you a lot during this difficult period and I would be glad to be able to comfort you. In any case, I am going to try to come see you both. That's something I think about every day.

I remember.

Pierre

He offered to pay her a sort of alimony. One hundred fifty francs a month. She accepted that amount without discussion. She received the check in the mail. He came to see me regularly, he picked me up when school was out, we would go away for the weekend that very evening or the next day. If he had a headache, he would book a room. He regularly stayed at the Hôtel de la Paix. On the second floor, the restaurant had an immense bird-cage along a whole section of wall. An aviary that decorated the room. It was very cheerful. We would dine with the chirping in the background and the view of the birds skipping from one little branch to another. In the morning we would leave. The next day he would bring me home in the car, or he'd leave me at a station and I'd take the train.

"Kiss your *maman* for me!"

She had been alone the whole weekend. She'd taken a drive in the city and had gone to see a film. The rest of the time, often, she had cried alone in the apartment. She was hanging onto a sentence written by Paul Guth that she had cut out of *La Nouvelle République* many years earlier: "Certain flops prepare distant victories." She'd put it in her wallet. There were other little clippings carefully folded in the pockets. Another one cut out on the day of my birth: "Children born today will have a fine intelligence and a generous and altruistic nature. Quite undisciplined and quick to revolt or get angry. They may succeed in original research and personal work. Strong ambition."

She had lost ten kilos. The only skirt that fit her was beige, flat across the stomach, with a box pleat in the front. The others hung from her hips.

Her room and mine were separated by a wall against which the heads of our two beds were placed. At night, before turning out the light, I would tap three little taps on the wall, she would reply with three identical taps.

The balcony faced north and overlooked a bypass. The rumble of the cars was permanent and reached our floor. It was cold out there. There was wind. We never used it. Sometimes at night she would get up. She'd put on her bathrobe and lean her elbows on the railing, watching the cars go by and crying. If she had stayed in her room, given the thinness of the wall, the noise of her sobs would have awakened me, on the balcony they were muffled and mixed in with the sonorous mass that rose from the bypass. But I could hear.

"Don't worry, go back to bed, my little fawn. It will be all right. It's the adjustment. It will pass, go back to bed. Go on, Christine, go back to your room. Go, go. You have to sleep. You have school tomorrow."

The first winter was very cold. In the mornings, in the parking lot, we scraped the frost off the windows of the car. During the quarter-hour drive to the center of town, we talked.

"Do you remember when you used to say to me: *You're cheerful, Mama*?"

"Yes."

"Well, I hope I'll be cheerful again one day."

"Me too, Mama."

"We have to hold on. Right, my little fawn? We must not get discouraged."

"Yes, Mama."

"It will be all right. Hmm? We just have to hold on."

In the evening I took the bus home, or I went to wait for her at the door of the Caisse. She was almost always late, I often ended up crouching on the sidewalk.

There was a large cultural center and sporting complex near us. It was composed of a Center for Youth and Culture, a skating rink, and an Olympic-size swimming pool. The theater had five hundred seats, the discotheque was lined with cork, it was warm, low-ceilinged, there was a cine-club, several exhibit walls in the mezzanine and the walkways, the cafeteria was at garden level and extended into a terrace open in the summer. The building was made of light-colored bricks. It wound around like a snail. One Sunday afternoon, we decided to go see a play.

"It was fantastic, Mama."

"We had a nice Sunday, didn't we?"

"It was brilliant."

"They don't have that at Châteauroux. We'll have to hold on, my little fawn, we'll get there."

We ate facing each other in the kitchen, she with her back to the window, me with my back to the room. We had endives with ham, pasta bakes, stuffed tomatoes, filets of fish. In memory of my childhood, she'd make me a semolina-tapioca cake from time to time. We watched television. We listened to music. Catherine Lara had just released her first record. There was a little fireside stool facing the record player in a corner of the living room, on which I would sit.

"Before dawn after the grand night

After we've made love and told each other everything

We say see you soon we say forever

In a month in a year

When will we see each other again?

But how far is that time

But how sweet was that love."

She crossed the room. "Oh yes, that! How sweet was that love. Good god. My god yes. How sweet was that love. Yes. Oh yes."

She sat down on the couch, she took her tube of cream, she

started massaging her hands. Palms, fingers, one by one, from her wrists to the tips of her fingernails, pulling her fingers. After the piece was over, she continued to sing. Her skirt rose up on her thighs. Her flesh flattened out on the cushions.

"Your thighs are all soft, Mama."

"Well thank you very much! You'll see, when you're my age, how yours will be too."

She was forty-three.

It was the chalky soil of the region, we had been told, that explained the yellow color of the cathedral. And it was also what made the vineyards exceptional. The vines were grouped on a hill called the "mountain of Reims." The hillsides were covered with them, except for a little forest on the western flank, "les Faux de Verzy." The *fau* was a variety of tree whose trunk was twisted, a bizarre cross between an oak and a beech tree, which grew only within this little perimeter. The paths were strewn with as many acorns as beech leaves. There was another possible walk, in the city along the canal. A dirt path followed the current until it came to a lock. Apartment buildings with little wooden balconies lined the water. They belonged to a residential area that rose up toward the basilica.

"I'm sick and tired, we don't do anything, we're bored to death. It's not interesting! What a bore! We just sit here, doing nothing. It's so boring! Life is just so not interesting! I'm bored here. What a bore!! What boredom! We never talk about any-thing. About anything interesting. I am sick and tired of this life, really I am."

Past the discovery stage, our tête-à-tête became difficult.

"I'm sorry, Christine, I can't offer you anything more than what I offer you. We can go for a walk, go to the movies. I can't do anything more. I admit it. I have my limits. I don't have your father's salary, nor his culture, I regret it. Do believe me. And I am surely not as interesting as he is, I grant you that. I too would like to be able to offer you things that interest you."

I would stay in my room until dinnertime. At the table, most often we were silent. Or we had arguments. If I returned from a weekend with my father, I told her about it.

"I would like to retain everything he tells me. Everything. Everything I learn, everything he explains to me. It's so interest-ing. If only I could retain everything! I can't even retain half of it, I retain … maybe a quarter, not even, a tenth."

At the office, they were waging war against her, between us it was difficult, she had no friends, no one to talk to besides her general practitioner.

"It's difficult, doctor … My daughter is an adolescent …"

"What is difficult, ma'am?"

"Oh, a number of things. We have lost our circle of acquain-tances, that's one thing. Okay, it was a family circle. Maybe it wasn't perfect, but it was an intimate circle. Protective. Here we have nobody. We don't have any close contacts. The people I work with … But that's quite external. I can't even say those are relations. It's very superficial. There is nobody whose house I can stop by, for example. Or even whom I could telephone. I need to talk sometimes, you see."

"Of course."

"I've been raising my daughter all by myself ever since she was born. It gives me great happiness but it's not always easy. So now she's met her father. That's a bit of a relief. But it's complicated. Okay. He's a very cultivated man who brings her many things. In comparison, I bring her nothing anymore. And she is sick and tired of her mother."

She described an evolution. It was adolescence. A normal evolution. Adapting to the city made things difficult. She couldn't gain back the weight she'd lost. She was sleeping badly. She recognized she was showing signs of depression. She seemed sad, her voice was calm.

"Sure, I can't bring her what her father brings her. What I offer is no longer enough, I understand that. So then there is the phenomenon of rejection. It's normal. But it's hard to live with."

"You say you understand it, ma'am?"

"Yes, I understand it."

"What do you mean? What do you understand?"

"I find it normal, in a way. And I would even say I accept it."

"Why do you accept it?"

"Her father is a person of great instruction. Much more than I am. They have a lot of tastes in common. For my daughter, inevitably, it's interesting. I find that normal. She had been deprived of it. She is drawn to what he offers her. I understand that. And I understand that what I can offer is not very much in comparison. I accept that. Yes. I am forced to accept that in any case. Do you think I have a choice, doctor?"

"I don't know, maybe."

"No, doctor, I don't think so. There is a separation, it's surely inevitable. What can I do? I'm not telling you it isn't making me suffer, okay ... I don't think I'm a stupid person, you know, doctor. But I don't have her father's culture. That's for sure. The conversations we have together, she and I, are simpler. No doubt. We have been very close, my daughter and I, you know. This makes for a huge change. She's not bored with him, that's good. With me now she gets bored. Okay, I understand. That makes me unhappy, I'm not going to say the opposite."

"Does she see him often, her father?"

"Regularly, yes. I'm glad about it, actually, that's not the question. I think it's wonderful that he can bring her so many things. He opens her up to a world she would never have known, and he is her father. This opening will be important for her later. He brings her an opening onto an enormous number of things. Which I don't know. And since those are things that interest her. Inevitably ..."

Sometimes my friend Véronique would invite me to her house. She was the daughter of a wine grower from Verzenay. There were three floors of living space, a hangar that housed a wine press, and a beautiful garden in the back. Rose bushes climbed on the façade around the stairs, the roses formed a sort of canopy above the stoop. She had caught sight of my father several times, she was curious about him. We were interested in the same things, literature, theater, and languages. When my mother came to get me, her parents invited her to sit in the living room, offered her a glass of champagne, and explained why the tulip-shaped glass she was holding in her hand allowed the aromas to spread and the bubbles to rise.

Had someone seen us in the kitchen, in the evenings, they could not have imagined how much I had loved her. There was no longer any intimacy between us. We were at daggers drawn. If she made a grammar mistake, I pinched my lips and my body stiffened on my chair. If she made a second one, I corrected her in a cutting tone.

The next day, in the car, it continued on a new subject.

"Oh come on, Christine, stop pushing and shoving me like that all the time. Why do you tell me things that hurt me like that?"

"Well it's true, that's all, I'm sorry! We are not a family."

"Oh yes we are! We are a family."

"Two people, that's not a family. I'm sorry."

"I disagree. We are a family of two people, but we are a family. What are we then if we're not a family?"

"A family is not this. For me, in any case, we are not a family. I'm sorry. It's the truth. I don't see why it's a problem to say it. You can't force me to think that we are a family. I have the right to believe we are not a family after all. And I have the right to say it."

"Oh sure, you, you of course, you have the right to say anything."

"We are a mother and a daughter, there, that's all. Two people in a house is not a family. I'm sorry."

Her tears started to flow. She was silent.

"I'm sorry, it's obvious. Not worth crying about."

My father no longer came into the building. When he brought me back, he dropped me in the parking lot. I took the elevator, I arrived on the sixth floor, and I rang the bell. She opened the door. I did not smile. I no longer leapt into her arms. I gave her two quick kisses on her cheeks in the entryway. I looked annoyed as if I regretted returning to my life with her.

We went to Châteauroux for the holidays. We went to see Rue de l'Indre again. And we walked into the lane in silence. Then we came to the house. The new owners had built a wall. We couldn't see anything. We could see the kitchen window because it opened into the lane.

"No, Christine, don't cry."

We couldn't see the garden. We stood on tiptoe. We could see the tops of the trees. On All Saints' Day we went to the cemetery. We put flowers on the little gray tomb where my grandmother and her grandmother were both buried. Her grandmother was called Marie. She didn't know how to read or write. At age ten, she had gone to work as a farm girl in an agricultural business in the area. Five years later she was expelled, pregnant by the owner. She had returned to Châteauroux. She had got married. Her husband had recognized my grandmother. In spite of her illiteracy, she was respected. She was quite a woman; you had to not tread on her feet. She and her husband ran a horsemeat butcher shop in the market. They had bought the house at 36 Rue de l'Indre. They owned all the land from the street to the river. They lived in the house with the little tower and received rent from a few tenants. At twenty, my grandmother had left for Paris. She had worked in a fashion house where she was a couturiere and then a fit model. She had been obliged to return because of a pulmonary congestion. She had met my grandfather on New Year's Day at a dance and had fallen madly in love with him.

A free newspaper landed in all the mailboxes in Reims. It gave the schedule of performances and published several columns of classified ads of which one was titled "personals." And she always bought *The French Hunter*. She liked one of the ads. She went to see the man in Paris, and she returned enchanted. A second visit was planned. When she returned, she was crying. It was a Sunday evening, I was just coming home, I had seen my father, she was sitting in the armchair near the balcony, with her back to the light.

"You know what? I tell you, life is really a dirty trick!"

A few days later, in the free newspaper of the city, an ad caught her attention: "Antiquarian would like to form a group of friends."

The meetings took place above the store. People spoke to each other using the familiar "tu." There was a group of five or six people. A woman of Flemish origin who lived alone with her two daughters. A chemical engineer from Mauritius who worked in a detergent factory. He dated a blonde girl with blue eyes and skin like a baby's, he was called Marc and the girl Amandine. An insurance employee who was interested in culture. He loved to laugh, he was twenty-seven, had a little lisp, theories on everything, and bright eyes.

"You're wearing beautiful velvet pants, I say, Rachel! This brown velvet is beautiful, matte. It's mysterious, bewitching, profound. I am looking for a jacket in navy blue velvet. And I'm not finding it. I want it to be a smooth, shiny velvet."

"You were saying you like matte velvet?"

"For brown velvet! Yes! It must be dull, opaque, faded, mysterious, profound. But for navy blue, not at all. Navy blue velvet should be sparkling, brilliant, like water. Sorry, I'm changing the subject, this week I had a rather traumatic experience. By chance I ran into a girl I had known very very well, in the street, I had heard that she had got married, I hadn't seen her since, I remembered she was a pleasant girl, who had a posterior ... let's say ... a friendly posterior! Well, when I saw her again, you would have said a basket for French fries."

The antiquarian: "Oh! Régis!"

After that the group divided into three cars headed for the Faux de Verzy. They went for walks, sometimes she would take me. And we returned just before dinnertime.

"He's not bad for a guy, this guy Marc, I think! He's a little young for me, too bad, I like him a lot. That's the type of man I like, but he's a little young ..." He was ten years younger than she was.

"In any case he's with Amandine, isn't he?"

"I'm just saying, given my age it would be ridiculous in any case. I'm not going to make any advances. If he was interested in me, on the other hand, maybe I wouldn't say no."

One Sunday after a trip, Marc took us home, he had a Ford Taunus in metallic blue. He came up to the apartment with us. The three of us sat in the living room.

A little book was lying on a low table.

"Aha, Scorpio!"

"Yes, Marc, I am a Scorpio, and I'm interested in astrology. Do you find that stupid?"

"The Scorpio woman and love, aha, aha …"

"What can I say, Marc, I'm interested in it. It's surely idiotic, but okay. It's ridiculous, right?"

"Not at all. On the contrary. It's very interesting. Let's see, let's see … The Scorpio woman is sentimental …"

"Hmm. Ye-e-s."

"The Scorpio woman is often frigid …"

"No …"

"Or a nymphomaniac."

"Not that either."

I was sitting beside her on the couch. He was in the armchair opposite.

My father invited me to spend a week with him in Strasbourg. His children still did not know of my existence, but they were leaving for Morocco with their mother for the Easter vacation. The apartment would be empty.

When I returned, she came to get me at the station. I smiled vaguely when the compartment door opened. Each time I came back to her, things didn't seem to go well. I stepped down onto the platform with my bag on my shoulder.

"How did it go?"

"Middling."

"Oh really? Why?"

I never made negative comments.

"Why middling?"

"It was difficult."

"Oh. What was difficult?"

"He was. He is difficult."

"But what? What in particular?"

"His personality."

"I know."

The conversation did not continue in the car. We arrived in Châtillons. And there, in the apartment, starting from a small point, from a way I had of talking to her, a comment, a more aggressive tone than usual to which she replied with aggressiveness, a crisis exploded. It finished in accusations. In shouting. Until we both began to cry, both of us exhausted. We kissed. Then she held me tight in her arms.

"It did not go well, Mama …"

"What happened? Did something particular happen?"

"Well, for example, one day, after lunch, we were going out for a spin. I was glad, because since he was working, I would wait for him all day, and now we were going out. So I was happy. I was glad we were going to go out. He was in the hallway and I joined him. I went out into the hallway. And I shut the door. At that moment he realized the key was inside. But I had shut the door, I thought he had taken the key. Since he was out in the hallway. There was no way I could know that it was still inside. And then, Mama, he began to accuse me. Mama, you cannot imagine the way he talked to me. He told me you don't close the door when you're not in your own home. That it wasn't done. That it was rude when you were at someone else's house. That it was impolite. That I shouldn't have done that, that I wasn't at my own home. Do you realize? Mama, do you realize how disgusting it was to say that, to say that to me! He talked to me like I was rotten fish. It was horrible. It lasted all afternoon. He kept shouting at me all afternoon. You cannot imagine, Mama, it was awful."

"It wasn't your fault, after all! You couldn't have known that he hadn't taken his keys."

"Right. But he kept saying it was my fault. Because …"

"Don't cry, Christine, it's over. Tell me about it calmly."

I went on. "Well, he said that … that when you are at someone else's house … Well, uh … That you don't go out first. But second. After the one who lives there. I said, 'Yes, but you were in the hallway.' He replied that had nothing to do with it. The fact that he was in the hallway changed nothing. That it was a matter of principle. That one doesn't close the door when one is not in one's own home. He said that I don't know how many times, Mama. That it was a matter of politeness, of education, that I should have known. That it's a rule. And all that. That I should have gone out second. After him. Because we were at his house. And not shut the door as if I were in my own home. So many times he said that to me. Do you realize. Do you realize how mean it was to say that to me, Mama? It was hard, all the same … to hear that. For me."

"Yes. Very hard. And how did all that end?"

"Well, he called in a locksmith, and it cost a lot. He said it was my fault. And the day was spoiled."

"And afterwards? Was it better? Or was it like that all week?"

"It wasn't very pleasant, as weeks go, Mama."

"It was too long, maybe. Don't you think?"

"Yes. Maybe. And also he went to work. While I stayed home all day, and I was bored."

"Yes, it was too long."

"And even, also, it wasn't good. Something else happened."

"What?"

"Well …"

"Tell me."

"Well … See, in the morning, he would leave early. I had my breakfast after he left. And then he returned at noon. One day at noon, he came back, and I had forgotten to put the milk bottle back in the refrigerator after my breakfast. When he saw that the milk was still on the table, you cannot imagine how he talked to me, Mama!!!"

"Because of a bottle of milk you didn't put away?"

"Yes. He talked to me like I was rotten fish. Like he hated me. Screaming. He said, 'Don't you know that milk goes sour?' And he shouted, 'You don't know that! How come you don't know that at your age?' The tone of his voice, his tone, Mama. It was horrible. It was horrible, Mama. He said things, some things, horrible things. Horrible. They were horrible things, Mama. Shouting, loud. Loud, loud. So loud. You don't know. You cannot even imagine. You cannot even imagine how loud he was screaming. 'Milk goes sour if you don't put it away, at your age you don't even know that?' And I said: 'Yes, I do know that, but I just forgot. I didn't think about it. I didn't do it on purpose. I'm sorry. I didn't notice.' And he: 'Stop crying like a little baby girl.' Because I was crying. I can't take it, Mama. I can't take it anymore. It was a hard week. It was too hard. It really didn't go well. Really not. It didn't go well at all. At all, at all."

"Will you want to go back there again, or not?"

"I don't know. Yes. Maybe."

"In any case, you surely shouldn't stay for so long."

"Oh, no, absolutely not."

"He has a terrible character. But there were some good moments even so? Or it was like that all the time?"

"Yes, there were some good moments. Yes. Even so. But not many. At the beginning. At the very beginning of the week. He is writing a book on the Iberian language … So he told me about it. And it was interesting."

"And otherwise, the apartment was nice?"

"Yes. It's pretty. It's very comfortable. It's well furnished. There are tons of little things, lots of little details, they're pretty."

"And in what style? Sort of old-fashioned? Sort of modern?"

"More old-fashioned. There is some old furniture, which comes from his family, I think. There are paintings on the walls, engravings. And I really liked the bathroom. It's very pretty. There are lots of glass pots with necklaces inside. Very fun, very colorful. And in the living room too, there are lots of little objects, it's cute …"

"Me I don't like things that are cute."

"But it's not *only* cute. There are some really beautiful pieces of furniture that come from his family, they are very beautiful. And they live right near the park of the Orangerie, in a townhouse. It's big. There is an immense bookcase that's two stories tall. And on the mezzanine level there is another little living room, a little reading room. Where you can also watch television. And in the bookcase, there is a whole section just with films. There are all the great films by all the great filmmakers. I really would have liked to have the time to watch them all. It was impossible, there were so many. It's a whole section of wall. They have a video recorder. So when films are on TV late at night, they record them. And he puts the corresponding article from *Le Monde* or *Télérama* with the videocassette. That way you can see the year it was made, the name of the author, everything. And outside the windows you can see the Orangerie. It's magnificent."

Summer was coming. One of my former friends from Châteauroux invited me for three weeks at the seaside in Vendée. It wasn't definite yet, there was work being done in their house. It was on the Atlantic coast. At Saint Jean de Monts, facing the beach. To go swimming you just had to cross the road.

Dear Rachel,
I am pleased that you are curious about my research about Iberia, unfortunately I have not had the time, these last few days, to indulge my avocation. As for the chapters that are done, as soon as I read them I want to add or remove something. However, since you've requested it so nicely, I will find the strength to renounce perfection and soon I will send you a few chapters.

You know that I have reserved the month of July for a vacation in Canada, which I have been dreaming about for years now. It's time I rid myself of my obsession. It seems a shadow is casting some doubt on Christine's plan to stay at the seaside. With all my heart, I hope the invitation extended to her will be confirmed. As for you, I am still hesitating, because it pains me to class you among the "French who will not have a vacation this year." That is why I would like you to answer this question: Where would you like to go if Christine leaves you to yourself? Spain, Tunisia, the Atlantic shore near our little girl?

If my finances do not prevent it, I could join together in one time the sums I plan to provide you over a period of several months. You should probe your own desires and perhaps the offers from travel agents.

Keep me informed about Christine's projects, your intentions, and also your health, about which you aren't breathing a word in your letter.

I am thinking of you.
Pierre

At the beginning of the month of June, my uncle, my aunt, and my cousins came to see us. We visited the cathedral. We went to Place d'Erlon. My uncle walked behind us with his eyes raised to the façades. My aunt, belted into a tight jacket, held a box of cakes dangling from a string. The baker had given her the change without looking at her, while speaking to another person. My mother explained the mentality of the people of the region, their coldness. I walked between them, and to amuse them, I imitated the Reims accent: "Ah wall, I dunnoh!"

At the end of the afternoon, my father telephoned. He was in Belgium and, rather than return directly home, he was proposing to swing by Champagne. The next day, around one in the afternoon, the doorbell rang. I went and opened it, I made the introductions. During lunch he was curious, he asked them questions, when it was time for dessert he realized he had forgotten his cigarettes in his car, he went down. My uncle said, "He's very nice."

I went into my room to get the photo of my half-brother and my half-sister, my uncle held it up beside my face, he noticed resemblances. My father came back up. He proposed to take me out for a drive, in the evening he brought me back. The whole family was gathered around the television, on the couch and the two armchairs, which had been moved closer.

My aunt got up. "So did you go to a restaurant?"

"Yes, the hotel restaurant."

"So that's the hotel he always goes to?"

"Yes, you know, the one where the restaurant has an aviary, I told you about it, yesterday we went by it, Place d'Erlon."

"I see."

After the summer vacation, Marc telephoned. I was alone in the house. The next day, he came to get me at school. A few days later he took me to his house. One Saturday night I stayed the whole night. And the next morning, to clarify the situation, he took me home, knowing she would be there.

A few months later, he called her at the Caisse. "We have to see each other, Rachel."

He proposed to stop by and pick her up that very evening.

She saw the Ford Taunus right away, parked along the sidewalk, from the inside he was holding the door open for her. Then things went very quickly. She sat down beside him. And in the car, parked there, they spoke.

"I have to tell you some things about Christine and her father. She absolutely must not go to Paris this weekend. It would be catastrophic for her. Because he has been sodomizing her for years."

It took her some time before she understood what was going on. And then it was like a blow to the head.

During the night that followed, she had a violent attack of fever. Her temperature rose to 105.8 degrees. She had an infection of the fallopian tubes. She was hospitalized, she stayed in the hospital for ten days. She was dumbfounded. At the same time … she was not surprised.

∽

I wrote my father that I didn't want to see him anymore.

Christine,
I have always respected your will and I will honor your new decision. What you told your mother is serious, it's a knife you are planting in my heart and I am going to have to recover from this wound. My disappointment equals the measure of joy I felt in meeting you. Getting to know you was a great happiness, but today I

have the feeling I was mistaken about you. Later, no doubt, you will
realize the pain you are inflicting on me.

I hope nevertheless that life will conform to your desires.

Papa

He continued to send her one hundred fifty francs once a month.

Two years later, a few days after my birthday, I had just turned eighteen, she received a letter, he informed her he was stopping the payments.

It was a clean cutoff.

"You know, Christine, if I had wanted to, I could have forced him to pay me a good alimony until you finished your studies. I would have had to go to court. And especially, I would have had to take care of it before you turned eighteen. It has to be done before a child reaches adulthood. Well. Now it's no longer possible. He's a clever one, Papa Angot, he knows what he's doing. He knows there's nothing I can do anymore. And I would have had much more than one hundred fifty francs if I had asked for alimony, you can be sure of that, given his position!"

"Why didn't you do it when there was still time?"

"Oh you know. No. No." She shook her head from left to right. "I didn't want to. No."

"Why?"

"No. No no. I never wanted to go there."

The corners of her mouth went down, indicating her scorn for what she could have done and that others in her situation would have done.

"It would have been normal, Mama. You should have. Even for me."

"I never asked him for money, I wasn't going to start."

"Why not?"

"No." She smiled, still shaking her head. "No no."

She kissed me. And she stroked my hair. "Oh la la, my little fawn."

The timbre of her voice was not the same as before. The words seemed to emerge from an ancient box, as if preserved there for several years, emerging one by one, detached from each other, without fluidity, like old papers that crumbled between her hands in the light.

"Oh. La la … My. Little. Fawn …"

She met a physics professor, he taught at the Université de Reims. He lived in Paris, he was married. A year later, he broke up with his wife and came to live in Châtillons. At the dinner table, we talked a lot about politics. He was militating for the SNESUP, a left-leaning syndicate of higher education teachers. I was studying law and I participated in the conversations. Then I left home. In the weeks that followed, she took in a little stray cat wandering in the neighborhood, which she called pussycat. She often called it little fawn and me pussycat. She spoke to it with the voice she had used to speak to me and in the same tone.

On my twentieth birthday, my uncle, my aunt, and my cousins came to Reims. She put out the silverware and fancy china. At dessert, the kitchen door opened, she was holding a cake, arms held high, twenty lighted candles illuminated her smile. Outside it was dark, and Marie-Hélène had turned off the lights. We could hear the cars going by on the bypass. And her, singing:
    "You aren't twenty every day
    It comes only once
    The day passes too quickly, alas
    That's why you have to take advantage of it
    It is the most beautiful day of your life ..."
    She walked in holding the cake up high, my uncle, my aunt, my cousins, and André, the physics professor, joined in the chorus: "It comes only once, you aren't twenty every day."
    She put the cake in front of me, standing behind my chair, she kissed me, leaning over my shoulder. "Huh, my little fawn. Your twentieth birthday is beautiful. You will see. You are going to have a beautiful life. Huh? You mustn't cry, Christine, huh? Don't cry, my pussycat."

Sometimes she would mention Charlie, her fiancé at seventeen.

Or Jean Dubois. When she talked about the past, her first loves, the passing of time. Then she glossed over several years and arrived directly at André. She thought they resembled each other.

"Oh la la, these Aquariuses!"

They got married one summer day.

I had just moved in with a guy, the son of the director of the Caisse. She moved into the same neighborhood with André. Our two apartment buildings were separated by a little alley. From the balcony of her kitchen, she could see my windows. We ran into each other every day, and we telephoned several times a day.

"So are you still seeing your acupuncturist?"

"Yes, but well … you know, Mama, I lived through some very hard things."

"But now you're fine with Claude."

She had known him a long time. When he was in high school, then a college student, he would go see his father from time to time at the Sécurité Sociale.

"You're okay, you two? It's over, all that. No? You're fine with Claude. Aren't you?"

"We love each other a lot, but it's not always easy. What I had to live through keeps me from living well."

"It's not getting better? You still think about it?"

"There are times when I feel like going to see my father and breaking everything in his house."

"Oh that … me too! But where would that get you?"

"I would like him to be conscious of the fact that he screwed up my life. That's all."

I don't know exactly what year it was, but sometime between my sixteenth and twenty-sixth birthdays, my father bought a pied-à-terre in Paris. The apartment was in the seventeenth arrondissement on the seventh and top floor of a Haussmann-era building at the corner of Rue Médéric and Rue de Courcelles. Several maid's rooms had been joined together, walls knocked down, a bathroom created, as well as a little kitchen. All together it was an ensemble of seventy square meters, ten minutes from Place de l'Étoile and an equal distance from Parc Monceau and Boulevard Pereire. His wife had turned it into a practical and comfortable place. The walls were painted white. There was only one splash of color, an immense patchwork quilt fixed to the mansard wall. The apartment was a harbor of calm. They would go there together or independently. He, quite regularly. She, a few days a year to see an exhibit and tour the city. Their children had grown, they went there also. The year I was twenty-six, after a ten-year interruption, I saw him again. He gave me a set of keys. When the apartment was free, I could go there.

I met his wife during a lunch there. A blonde with long hair and a big nose. The three of us were sitting at the round table which was covered with a white tablecloth. The folds fell to the floor. All the dishes were white. The plates, the platters, the coffee cups, the butter dish, the sugar bowl, etc. Turning toward me, she smiled and told me about the first time she had lunched at the home of my father's parents. A Sunday, Boulevard Pereire.

"Dey adoret oysters, you know ... Dey vere connoisseurss. Und for dem, you see, it vas an effent, dat day. For me too, actually. Opfiously. Pierre vas introducink me to dem. I vas tventy. I vas fery intimitated. I vanted to make a goot impression, you see. I vas fery younk, fery timit. Und dere ver oysters, opfiously. Und denn sometink happened – incredible. An incredible tink! Vich had neffer happened to dem or anyvone in deir family. Und it hass neffer effer happened to me again since. In duh first oyster I picked up vit my fingerss, Christine, und put in my mout, I felt a little piece dat crunched between my teet. I didn't dare take it out. Before svallowing it. So I vouldn't look like I had bad mannerss, you understand. I didn't vant to put my fingerss in my mout. But I did anyvay. Because I didn't know vat it vas. I was fery embarrassed, opfiously. Vell! You know vat it vas?"

"No."

"It vas a pearl, Christine! Dere vas a pearl in dat oyster! Can you imagine? It's incredible, no?"

"Yes, it's rare."

"A pearl. A gray pearl. It's incredible. No? It vas a magnificent omen. Don't you tink? I shouldn't say 'don't you tink' in front of Pierre. He issn't going to be happy. Right, darlink? But anyvay, it's incredible. Isn't it?"

"Yes, it's beautiful."

"Anyvay, I kept it. Ven you come see us in Strasbourg – because you vill come, I hope – I vill show it to you if you vant."

My father got up. There were two white couches facing each other. He sat down and opened his newspaper.

"Christine, I vant to tell you sometink, but I don't know if I dare. You know, sometimess, I am troublet. Becausse I tell myself I repeated, against your modder, de fiolence de Germanss dit to de Chewss."

"How so?"

"Becausse I married your fadder. And your modder had a chilt vit him. And she vas all alone. And she vas so in lofe. She vas fery much in lofe vit him, vasn't she?"

"I think she was."

"She vas fery beautiful. Vasn't she?"

"Well, when I was little and she came to get me at school, I was very proud."

"I hafe seen photos. She vas fery beautiful. I hafe kept them, I hafe photos of almost all the vomen Pierre hat before me. I also hafe photos of Françoisse, Brichitte, Frida. Your modder vas the most beautiful, I believe. She must still be fery beautiful."

"Yes."

"So I vas sayink, I hafe de impression I vas redoink dis fiolence against your modder, who vas Chewish. The humiliation. Dat de Germanss dit to de Chewss. I vas fery uncomfortable."

My father looked up from his newspaper, he gave her a sign of disapproval. By laying his head on one side. She changed the subject.

"Vat are you two goink to do tomorrow? I'm goink back to Strasbourg. But you? You could go to de Salon du Lifre! It's right nearby. You can valk dere. It might be interestink for Christine."

My mother was in Paris that weekend, we met by chance in a walkway of the Grand Palais. They said hello. She was with André. I made a comment to ease the tension. They laughed. Then said goodbye. They never saw each other again.

Back in Reims, I repeated to her what my father's wife had said about her guilt as a German with respect to her, who was Jewish.

"Oh yes, she said that?"

"Yes, yes. She dared. Yes."

"And otherwise, what's she like?"

"Average height, thin, blonde, long smooth hair, a big nose, her features sort of sharp, not very pretty but not bad. But stupid. Really stupid."

"She has pretty hair, I think."

"Sort of. Her hair is blond, fine, nothing special."

"You father had told me she has very pretty hair."

"Yes, okay."

And I told her the story about the pearl in the oyster.

From time to time, she still had moments of melancholy. Sometimes crying spells. She would speak of her dissatisfaction. But it would pass. A new cinema opened Place d'Erlon, with three big theaters. On Friday nights, she would meet André, they'd go see a movie then have dinner at the Continental. The population in Reims was starting to diversify. They had some friends. The autoroute was being built, the first section made it possible to get to Paris in an hour and a half. The beaches of the North Sea were accessible in less than three hours.

She lived in Reims until her retirement. I left after I finished school. And, with the distance, we were no longer in constant contact.

I was in Nice for the first years. At the airport, when the arrival gates opened, as soon as I saw her appear I threw myself into her arms.

"Mama, you are magnificent."

Seeing her was emotional. My back shook jerkily, and I put my head on her shoulder. I sobbed, we hugged.

"Don't cry, Christine, or you're going to make me cry. We're not going to cry, now. It's good to see each other again. It's fun. Right? Huh?"

"I love you, Mama, you know it."

"Me too, my little fawn."

I kept a diary for a few months, and one day, in the plane from Nice to Paris, I wrote: *Mama and André will be at Orly and we will have dinner together. Afterwards, it might be a little hard to sleep in the apartment that my father lets me use on Rue Médéric, where my memories are not all good ones. On the contrary. Far from it.*

We've landed. It's fine. I'm getting ready to see Mama's face. Her mouth, her sweetness, yes, it's just as expected. Mama, I love you.

We have dinner together. We enjoy it. Outside, it's cold. André is driving and we get a little lost looking for Rue Médéric in the dark. We park. They come up to the apartment with me to make sure everything is fine. Mama is concerned about the condition of the pipes and the smell of gas in the kitchen and the toilet. They leave. I'm not so uncomfortable as all that. It's fine.

Five after midnight, the telephone rings. My father. "I'm calling to welcome you."

Always turning things into a joke. We hang up, then it rings again. He had forgotten to tell me about a problem with the toilet, the reason for his first call.

I call Claude so his voice will be the last one of the day. I try to sleep. Not easy. Three o'clock in the morning, I call him: "Darling, I can't sleep, I'm scared."

"No no, you'll see, everything will be fine."

Finally I fall asleep.

My father and his wife waited until their children passed their baccalaureate exams before letting them know of my existence.

They wanted to meet me. The boy was spending his vacation on the Côte d'Azur, he phoned me. And we agreed on a rendezvous.

"So did he come?"

"Yes."

"How did it go?"

After a moment of silence, I said: "It didn't go at all. He rang the intercom, but I didn't open the door."

"What do you mean?"

"Well, I didn't answer. He rang, but I didn't answer."

"Really? But you had arranged to meet, he must have guessed you were there."

"Yes."

"And you didn't open the door?"

"No …"

"Did you say something to him on the intercom?"

"I didn't answer, I'm telling you."

"You didn't want to see him?"

"I don't know. I couldn't answer. That's all."

"You changed your mind at the last minute?"

"I don't know. I just can't explain it."

"You didn't answer at all! You didn't tell him anything, at all? He must have wondered. He must have rung again."

"Oh yes. As for ringing again. He rang again. He rang again a lot, even. He stayed downstairs a long time."

"Really?"

"Oh yes, a very long time."

"He wanted to meet you, it's too bad."

"That's how it is."

"Well, okay. Too bad. But if you couldn't answer."

"The first time, I didn't answer. He waited, and then he rang again. The second time I didn't answer either. He rang again, I still didn't answer. Things went on like that for about an hour. Before ringing again he waited, a long time or a short time. I was afraid he'd come up to my floor and hear noises. I stayed quiet. I didn't dare go out all afternoon. I was afraid he was still down there. I was having a bad time. My heart was beating fast. It was horrible. Thankfully Claude was there with me."

"And what was he saying, then?"

"Nothing. He was with me."

"You should have answered, Christine, really ... Don't you think?"

"Do you understand what it means, when I tell you I couldn't? I was paralyzed. In a state of panic. Do you understand?"

"Of course I understand."

"He rang he rang he rang like an animal. One time he kept his finger on the button for at least five minutes. Ten minutes, I don't know. Of course he knew I was there. But besides that, there are so many things he doesn't know. It was horrible, this awful riiiiiiiiiiiiiiiiiing. This awful riiiiiiiiiiiiiiiiiing that wouldn't stop."

"It's not his fault, you know."

"One time he made it ring for a long time. He kept his finger on the button for … oh, I don't know, maybe a quarter hour … Well, I don't know, maybe not, in any case it seemed very long to me."

"How long did he stay down there?"

"About an hour, I told you."

"Poor guy."

"Oh come on, listen, how can you say that? Did I hear right? You can't say that to me!"

"It's true, Christine, after all."

"So feel sorry for him."

"That's not it … But he was there, he came, he wanted to see you, he didn't know what was going on."

"Yeah, you're right. Okay. It's true. He's the one we should feel sorry for. No, it's true, he's the one who's a poor guy. Poor guy, poor little guy who spent an hour in the street when no one answered him. Such an injustice."

"That's not what I'm saying, Christine. Maybe you would have been glad to get to know each other. Both of you. You might have had some things to say to each other, no?"

"It's a little more complicated than that, you know … He rang he rang he rang he rang and the more he rang, the less I could open the door, anyway. It was more horrible for me than for him. You understand? I may well have wanted to be able to open the door for him. But I couldn't. The more he rang, the less I could, anyway. That's how it is."

"For sure, it's not easy. But what could he understand? He mustn't have understood what was happening."

"Well, he'll just have to find out."

"It would have been good if you'd opened the door for him, that's all I'm saying. You couldn't. And after a while, it was too late, but ..."

"Whose side are you on, now? Are you on my side or are you on his side? I couldn't answer."

"I'm on your side, Christine. Come on. You know that, for sure. Huh? You know that. Of course."

"So stop saying things that tell me you don't understand. Try to understand. Please. I need it. Try to be on my side. Really on my side."

"I don't need to try, Christine, really, I am on your side."

I would sometimes hang up on her. She would call back. I lifted the receiver so it would stop ringing and slammed it down on the phone. Sometimes I was the one who called back. We always ended up calling each other back. One or the other. After crying, each of us, by ourselves. And we spoke to each other calmly.

"I love you, Mama."

"Me too."

The year I was pregnant, I was expected to deliver on July 23. Claude was giving exams, he was going to be away the whole month. She rented an apartment in Nice. When my waters broke on the 8th, she and André took me to the clinic. I was given a room and she stayed beside me while waiting for Claude (who had been alerted) to get there.

The resemblance between her and my daughter struck me right away. I slipped my hand into the cradle and put it underneath her little face. I concentrated on her forehead, her gaze. It was the same mixture of depth and radiance.

"She has the same eyes as you do, Mama."

Then I lived in Montpellier.

Mama,

I love you. I think about you a lot, a lot, a lot. Here we are happy, life is simple, gentle, it flows. Léonore is a treasure, and, I think, an extraordinary little girl, extraordinary in her sweetness, her grace, a queen. For two months I have been trying to write a book which would be like a long letter in which I would talk to you. I'm having a hard time with it. I often cry. I don't know what will come of it, maybe nothing will come of it. I've fortunately reached an end. Talking about you had started to make me suffer, especially talking

about our love, about the image I have of you, made of memories,
expectations, so much happiness. I hope you will continue to love me.
You must. Léonore calls me 'Mama,' actually she says 'Momo,' she's
starting to say 'Papa,' she imitates dogs barking and cats meowing
when we see them. I'm very tired from stopping the medication, but
I'm trying to manage. When I think I'm going to be thirty-five next
year! I'm really right in the middle between Léonore and you. Not a
day, not an hour, goes by where I don't think about you.

    I give you a great big kiss.

    You are my maman.

    Christine

She left her job at the Caisse a little before the retirement age. She
had made the required number of years of contributions. She was
thrilled with the idea of getting up whenever she felt like it from
now on. They moved to Montpellier. She looked after her grand-
daughter and once again we were living in the same city. We went
out together, we went shopping, we dropped in at cafés. There
were broad luminous squares, bordered with cafés, where the
sun shone brightly.

    "I want to have a different life, I can't go on like this. Our life
is pleasant, but … I love Claude. But I don't think I want to stay
with him. I want to have a different life. I can't go on like this."

    "Meaning you can't go on like what?"

"I don't love him enough. I love him a lot. I love him, I'll always love him. No doubt I'll love him my whole life. It's even quite certain. But I am not 'in love' with him."

"But you say you will love him your whole life. What are you calling 'in love'? What do you mean? Don't you get along?"

"We do. But. I don't know … I'm not in love with him. I've never been in love with him. He's a wonderful man, whom I love, but I am not in love with him. There. That's all. I can't help it."

"You don't think it could be a passing thing?"

"No, I don't think so."

"Okay. If you're sure …"

"It's crazy how each time I tell you something, it can never be accepted as the truth. Never. It always has to be a 'passing thing,' or it has to be relativized in some way. I really don't know why I'm talking to you. What's the use of talking to you? You always have to take the opposite tack."

"That's not it, Christine. I'm worried about you. That's all. Claude has given you so much support. Even with your writing. Are you going to find anyone who will understand you as well? Who will support you, in that regard. That's it! That's it, that's what worries me. You understand? Did you think about it?"

"I don't want to be locked into that anymore. Whatever the reason may be. That's just it, it's only writing that makes me really happy. This can't last. I can try to have a life … I'm thirty-eight. I can try. And also, I can't stand this city anymore. I can't stand these people …"

"Don't you want to think it over a little, still? Claude has always backed you up so well. He's a sincere person, he loves you. He's amazing. He's not just anybody. I'm afraid you won't find someone who will support you as well. That's all I'm saying."

"Stop. Please. I can't believe how you always demoralize me like that."

"That's not my intention, Christine."

My father died. He had Alzheimer's. I hadn't seen him for ten years. I had been separated from Claude for a year. I learned of my father's death by a telephone call from my half-brother. The next day I was going up Rue de la Loge toward Place Jean Jaurès, she was going down in the opposite direction, toward Place de la Comédie. We bumped into each other.

"How are you?"

"Not too good. You see, I was expecting it, Mama, but it was a shock to find out he died. And you? Were you shocked?"

"No."

"It didn't trouble you?"

"No."

"Not at all?"

"No, Christine, it doesn't affect me."

"You're not sad?"

"No. I'm not upset."

"At all?"

"No."

"I don't get it. I am upset, in spite of everything. You're not upset? You're not sad at all? You don't feel anything?"

"No, Christine."

"Are you happy?"

"I'm neither happy nor unhappy."

"I'm having trouble understanding you. As for me, I don't know what's going on with me anymore. I was waiting for this death. And even dreamed about it. Now here it is. I thought I would be happy, the fact is I am not. Well, I don't know. I feel lost. I did cry, actually. You didn't? You loved him, though! This is a person you loved!"

"Yes. That's just it. I cried so much for him. I think I'm out of tears for him. I had already cried a lot before."

"I would like to go to the funeral. But not all alone. And I don't see who I can go with. No one has offered to go with me anyway. It's too hard by myself. I couldn't stand to be with all those people. Before, I would dream of this funeral. I would imagine his family crying, in a church, and me in the back, taunting them, and following them to the cemetery, I might have said something. I was waiting for this moment. And in the end, you see, it's more complicated. I don't understand how you don't feel anything. You feel nothing? You don't have any feelings? At all? At all at all? Positive, negative, nothing? … So then I really am all alone, aren't I? Once again. I'm going through a hard patch now. You see. All alone, as usual. Well, listen, I'm not thanking you, eh!"

I took a step forward to leave her and continue my walk. She held me back.

"Now you listen to me, Christine, I'm going to tell you something: If your father, even dead, can still separate us, that's no good."

"That doesn't mean a thing, it really doesn't mean a thing, you're just thinking of yourself. There was no one to protect me when I met my father. Now there is no one to help me live through his death. Look. Our relationship is screwed. Okay?! Goodbye. I'm going home now."

In the years that followed, I began to attribute my failures to her. I accused her of not having examined her conscience, of having stayed in analysis only three years, of having found an easy guilty party in my father, of not having reflected on her own responsibility for what had happened to me. As a consequence, I advised her not to be surprised about the difficulties our relationship had fallen into. I told her I was the victim of their shared egotism. That they were the same, in that respect. Preoccupied exclusively with their involvement with each other. That the famous photograph taken in the countryside, in the same position, leaning against the same post, was the proof of it. That they had each taken themselves as the mirror of the other. That I had been sacrificed to that.

"So now, I can't take it anymore. It's too hard. My life is too difficult."

"It'll be alright, Christine, I understand how you can be thinking that. Life can be difficult, very difficult. It won't always be like that. Life changes. I promise you. You'll see. You think everything is stuck sometimes ... But it isn't. It's not true. You think that, but it's wrong. You feel like you are in a tunnel, you tell yourself you're never going to get out. I understand how you can see things that way, but ..."

"No, you don't understand."

"I probably don't understand exactly ..."

"It's not that you don't understand exactly, it's that you don't understand a thing! You don't realize the difficulty. You don't know me. You don't know who I am."

"Why are you rattling me like this?"

"I'm just telling you the truth, that's all."

"I was certainly wrong, I don't deny it. But I'm not saying anything wrong now, Christine!"

A leaden weight was suspended above our heads, permanently. Its height varied. Its presence prevented us from breathing.

Sometimes it came crashing down on us. We could no longer pretend.

Physical proximity was no longer possible. The closeness, breakfasts, mealtime habits, seeing her in her bathrobe, watching the television news together. All that was over. It had disappeared. I was living in Paris with my daughter. She would come see us. She slept at our house only when I was away; as soon as I returned she went to a hotel. To avoid cohabitation, intrusions. The handling of our laundry, napkins, sheets, the sight of cotton pads for removing makeup, of leftovers in the refrigerator. We had no meals together at home. One evening, however, out of guilt, I asked her to stay for dinner. We set the table in the kitchen. We turned on the oven to heat up a gratin of pasta and some vegetable dishes, which she had prepared knowing I was coming home. I don't remember where I was coming from, I must have had something to do in another city, and she had come to look after my daughter. The places were set. We sat down. And we started to serve ourselves. All of a sudden I got up.

"I'm sorry, I can't stand it. It's just too much for me. Sorry. I'm tired, I'm sorry. I can't. Sorry, Léonore. I'm very sorry. I can't continue to chat like this, now, it isn't possible. It's not possible for me. Pretending, I just can't anymore."

"We are not pretending, Christine."

"Yes we are. We are pretending, Mama. At any rate I am pretending. And it's exhausting me. We're in a vacuum, we have nothing to say to each other. I can't stand it. I'm sorry, Léonore. I also would have wanted it to be possible, for us to have dinner, the three of us, with your grandmother, in peace. But it's not. It's not always easy, you know, relationships, even with people you love. You were glad to have dinner tonight with your grandmother, I know, and I'm asking you to forgive me, my little fawn, because I just can't. I'm sorry, my little kitten. I need to rest. To relax. I'm tired tonight. I can't force myself to have empty conversations like this. Mama, would you come with me, please?"

I walked out of the kitchen, she got up from the table and joined me in the corridor. We went toward the entryway. Once we were in front of the door: "Will you please leave, Mama. I'm sorry, this is all I can do. I am very sorry. But I can't handle it. Maybe one day things will be better. But now I want you to leave. Please."

"Of course, Christine."

"I'm very sorry."

"Don't be sorry, Christine, it's no problem."

Her coat was in the entryway, lying on a bench. She picked it up and put it on. I opened the door. She went out on the landing. I stayed on the threshold until the elevator arrived.

"I'm sorry, Mama."

"Don't apologize Christine. It's nothing serious. You'll rest. We'll see each other tomorrow … If you want. As you wish. Don't worry. Get some rest."

She always reserved a room in a little hotel near Place de Clichy. When she arrived at the ground floor of the apartment building, she went off in that direction. Without even looking up to see if I was on the balcony. Her silhouette disappeared at the corner of the street. I joined my daughter in the kitchen.

We made plans to meet in a café. Or she came to pick me up at home and we went out without taking the time to sit down in the living room.

As soon as she arrived I looked for the best way to cut it short. We no longer hugged each other. We kissed on both cheeks. We no longer sobbed while embracing. Sometimes André came with her. She had one hand on her phone while they were out. If I called she could feel it vibrate. And if I said I had time, we would meet. André went back to the hotel to wait for her.

She usually stayed for a week. We saw each other once at the beginning, once in the middle, once at the end.

When she had returned to Montpellier, I would call her. Sometimes I was in tears.

"There's only one thing I want. To kill myself."

"Don't say that, my Christine."

"Why shouldn't I say it? You think it isn't true? You think there isn't a reason to? There were things you should have done if you didn't want me to come to this. You have never done anything to try to understand your role in this whole affair. Look, I can't even manage to have a proper love relationship. You think one can cope after living through what I lived? Do you really think that? Are you aware that you are at the center of this business? . . . And that you never called yourself into question. Don't you understand, don't you understand the exorbitant space you take in my life, don't you understand that you have invaded my life? . . . That I can't live my own life. That for me everything revolves around you so much that I'm constantly looking for you. Always. Trying to be you. Oh yes! You're not aware of that, are you, huh? I've never sought out people I like myself. Just people you liked, or would have liked. I've never done anything except as a function of you. And here you are, never asking yourself any questions. No, I must be dreaming."

"I went to see a psychoanalyst for three years, Christine."

"Three years! You must be joking. What would you have the time to understand in three years?"

"Maybe that's not very long, but ... I did understand certain things, however. For example, when Marc came and talked to me, and afterwards during the night I had that infection ..."

"Oh give me a break."

She considered that the infection of her fallopian tubes, which occurred the night after Marc talked to her, had been a form of protection she was granting me. Because she had been hospitalized and I had to stay in Reims, whereas it had been planned that

I would go see my father. She was revisiting the decisive moments. Perhaps she had been wrong to listen to the advice society provided at the time. On the question of the equality of rights, for example. She had surely made some mistakes. She had probably lacked lucidity. She had certainly discharged herself from her responsibility for me when I met my father, believing she could do so after all those years.

"No doubt that was very selfish, right, but I think it was a factor."

Weeks in advance she talked about what we would do when she returned. She returned. We saw each other like two strangers who have nothing to say to each other. The meetings were formal, lifeless, focused on concrete matters.

"I'm telling you I can. I have some money I'm not using in my savings account. I can very easily give you some. Don't worry. In my mind, that was what I was intending in any case. You need a washing machine, don't you? Okay well, I can very easily buy you one. I have the right to give you a washing machine, don't I?"

Sometimes she arrived with a gift. It would be no good. The color, the shape, the material, the style. There was always something that wasn't right.

"You can exchange it if you don't like it, all right? I asked about it, you can do that."

In winter she gave me wool and silk shirts. Even if I didn't like them, they would be useful.

"You wear that under a sweater, it's good protection from the cold."

"Thank you."

"It's a little like I'm holding you in my arms, you see …"

I had stopped calling her Mama. It happened just like that, all by itself, without my intending it, without my deciding. Little by little. It was not premeditated. At first, the frequency of the word had gone down. As if it were no longer necessary. Then it had taken on an embarrassing tonality. It had become bizarre, disconnected. Then it had disappeared. Totally. It had become impossible for me to pronounce it.

As for her, she continued to use it. Regarding my grandmother. "I am afraid I wasn't kind enough to Mama."

"Why do you say that?" There were tears in her eyes. At first, a reflection at the back of her eyes, a vague liquid. It could have been a reaction of her cornea to a bit of dust. Or an illusion on my part.

"I was a problem for her."

"How were you a problem for her?"

"Because I stayed attached to your father, I believed in him for too long. I was unhappy. And I annoyed her with that."

It turned into a tear bath. Her cheeks were drenched. Her face began to grimace.

On the phone I would say hello and then start complaining

right away. My tiredness, my work, my solitude, the fact that I would never succeed. I'd call her out of a sense of obligation. When we hung up, we didn't know when we would speak again. But maybe the next call would be less tense.

On Mothers' Day, late in the morning, her telephone rang.

"Happy Mothers' Day."

"Thank you, my little fawn."

"I hope you are going to have a nice day."

"We'll try."

"What are you going to do?"

"I think we're going to the movies."

"What are you going to see?"

Scarcely had we begun a subject of conversation than I wanted to get on with the next one, or brutally say goodbye. Sometimes I would hang up all of a sudden without allowing her the time to finish a sentence she was in the middle of.

"Okay, hugs and kisses, see you later."

I would usually announce right from the start of the call: "Okay, I don't have a lot of time. But we can talk for five minutes."

She was no longer calling me of her own accord, she was afraid to call at a bad time. Except when an objectively long time had passed. She would leave a message on my answering machine. She would speak to the machine in a cheerful tone. She would make an effort to lighten her tone and speak with a cheerful voice.

"Okay well, it's me."

Before hanging up, she would raise the tone of the last part of her sentence.

To make sure she wasn't disturbing me, she got in the habit of sending texts to my mobile phone. Months would pass without our hearing each other's voices.

When I had a rendezvous, and since I'm always early, if there were a few minutes to kill before the person arrived, I would call her.

"Am I disturbing you?"

"No. You're never disturbing me."

When the person arrived, I would say goodbye and hang up, happy to be rid of the call. It was done.

If there was an emotion that surfaced, neither one of us would speak it aloud. As if nothing was there. There was almost no laughter either. When we met, she was tense. She tried to hide her anxiety. She would arrive in the café with a fake liveliness on her face. And she would sit stiffly in the booth.

"So? How are you?"

"Oh fine. And you?"

She would give me the news from Châteauroux, then look for another subject. The time dragged on. At times I would brutally interrupt her.

"Talk to me about your Jewishness."

She would relax. In the booth, her back would slump, apparently I was interested in that.

We were at the mercy of the ether, the mood, the moment, the ambiance, the subject – and the whole game would replay the next time.

But when she arrived, you had to see her walk to the table. She had the same smile as before, the same sparkling eyes. None of that had changed.

"You are magnificent."

What happened afterwards was a surprise.

Very old feelings, which we thought were lost, which dated from her youth and from my childhood, began to reappear. We were not expecting that. We no longer hoped for it. It happened without our realizing it. Over the years. Little by little. The pockets of anguish were still there. They could burst open at any moment. Attack us, pollute the atmosphere and the moment. They had become more rare, less powerful. At the start, there was a circumstance. After which things began to tip in the other direction. It did not present itself as a change, at the beginning. There was a circumstance, a simple circumstance that provoked a slippage. A very slight difference. A change of tone, first of all. Something infinitely small.

A long period without contact had passed and I had just gone abroad for two weeks of vacation. I decided to send her an email. It was not usual for us. Then I went out to dinner with the person who was with me, Charly, who had been sharing my life for several years. She replied the next day.

Your message moved me. I wanted to tell you that I love you too and I send you a big kiss.
See you soon, my Christine,
Mama

We wrote each other through the entire duration of this vacation.

Things are okay, but it's not easy. It has become necessary for me to accompany André for the slightest activity, dentist, errands … This requires my constant attention and presence. He forgets the code for the debit card, forgets the schedules. He leaves, and he returns with completely useless or unwanted things. Or he gets lost, all of a sudden he doesn't remember where he is.

It's okay, but it takes my attention and my presence. It's quite burdensome. It's not easy. Things are stable. But how can I put it … I feel like life is shrinking, that the possibilities are diminishing.

Anyway, so many people are living through more serious things that I'm trying to get along with this. It's a new perception of things.

I am very glad you are coming soon to Montpellier. In the meantime I wish you a good rest of your vacation.

Best wishes to Charly.
I give you a kiss.
Mama

André was undergoing treatment for a cancer that was destroying the protective envelope of his neurons. Certain connections no longer worked inside his brain. From one minute to the next he forgot what they had done, what they had said to each other. I called her that very evening.

Christine,
Yesterday evening on the phone, when I told you that I've been feeling alone ever since André's problems set in, you said, "We are alone." I replied, "It's true, but sometimes we think we aren't." I thought about it again this morning. Because you also said to me, "But he is there with you." Those simple words made me feel better. It became clear to me that even when we feel solitude, it's often false. Someone you love and who loves you, who is there through his presence or his speech – that represents life. Okay, maybe what I'm telling you doesn't make sense, but I wanted to say it.

I hope you have had a chance to relax and go out. Here, the weather isn't lending itself to that, it's been raining all day today.

I send you a great big kiss.
Mama

I've just read your text, Christine. I was intending to answer your email, of course. I wanted to do that today. I sometimes don't open my computer for several days. You can be sure that my reply, a little late, is not due to indifference – on the contrary, I liked your email – but to the need to gather my wits about me in a more auspicious environment than the hospital, before I replied to you. Yesterday, I spent a large part of the day there, André had an appointment for an assessment at the university hospital. They have a department that specializes in problems he's encountering. It's another world, not very pleasant. We go back there on Wednesday.

This evening, a little change, we are going to the Corum concert hall to hear Beethoven's ninth symphony, you know: Pah pah pah pah …

As you can see, there are still some good moments, luckily.

I hope things are going well for you two.

I am thinking of you and wish you nice days in your beautiful environment. Just reading your messages makes me envious. Take advantage of it.

I send you a kiss.

Mama

It's true, you are right, I was getting the numbers mixed up, pah pah pah pah is Beethoven's Fifth. The Ninth is the Ode to Joy, it was magnificent yesterday, really. A moment of pure happiness. When you hear that, you know that beauty exists.

Today is Didi's birthday, seventy-four. I remember her as a child, all round and pudgy, with her braids wrapped around her head. How time passes!

You ask me to tell you about the hospital … Yes, it's another world. A different world. The place where we go is special. It's involved only with problems related to "aging." The word alone suggests nothing pleasant.

You meet people there who walk with difficulty using a walker, etc. So you can picture the atmosphere.

But I don't want to sadden you today. Enjoy your last days in the sun.

I send you a kiss,
Mama

I have just received a nice message from Jean Dubois, signed "Your friend Jean." I was pleased.
Mama

You're asking me difficult questions, Christine. Can one explain feelings and the desire to have a child, I don't think so. You experience them.

Why I remained attached to your father for such a long time? A question I too can ask myself. I don't know how to answer. Reasons and explanations – there could be a lot of them. Life in Châteauroux, the social context at the time, the lack of new interesting people …

I don't very much want to dwell on it.
I send you a great big kiss, Christine.
Mama

A few months later she came to see me in Paris. We arranged to meet at a restaurant. It was a beautiful day and very hot. It was summer. The terrace was crowded. Inside it was empty. I took a table there. The moment she entered, I got up.

"You look great, you are magnificent."

"And yet, I slept badly."

We gave each other kisses on each cheek and she sat down opposite me.

"How are you?"

"Fine, but oh, our room was freezing. I don't know how they regulate their A/C. I was so cold I slept in my bathrobe."

"You should have called the front desk and complained."

"Oh no. They promised to lower it tonight."

"Yes, but it's not okay, you can't spend a whole night in the cold, you have to speak up. You are eighty-three years old! And André is ninety! You can't sleep in the cold."

The server arrived, we placed our orders. There we were facing each other in the practically empty room.

"Oh, I have something to show you!"

She picked up her bag, took out an envelope, slid out a photo which she placed on my napkin.

I lowered my head.

"Oh no, oh no, I'm putting it back then!!" I had burst into tears. "I don't want you to cry." With a quick, abrupt gesture, she took the photo back.

"Show it to me again, please."

She put it in front of me.

It was a photo of her with a young man. He had his hand on her shoulder. He was looking at the lens. With an incredible smile. The photo had been taken in the summer. She was wearing a printed cotton dress. He had on a white shirt hastily stuffed into his pants. The young man's radiance was striking. His air of swimming in happiness. Seeing the photo, one said to oneself, "It's not possible to be happier."

I started to cry again.

"That's me with Charlie."

"I know. I understood. That's just it."

The server brought our meals. She put the plate with the salmon in front of me and the other plate in front of her.

She took back the photo. She put it in her bag.

"Bon appétit, mesdames."

We thanked the server. We looked at each other. Our meals started to get cold on the table.

"You want to know what made me cry?"

"Of course, yes."

"You had always told me, when you spoke of Charlie, that you didn't like him. That you broke your engagement with him for that reason. And now I don't understand. I see a young man who is magnificent, who has an incredible smile, who is so beautiful … So beautiful … It's unreal."

Her eyes began to shine, she had a mischievous little smile. "You thought he was ugly?"

"You had told me you didn't like him, you always said that to me. You had told me you didn't like it when he kissed you. And now, I see this photo, with this young man whom I find magnificent. I didn't know he was so handsome. He was *very* handsome, this Charlie."

"Mostly he was very nice!"

"Yes, that you always told me. But you didn't tell me he was handsome. Not to that degree. On the contrary. Since you had told me you didn't like him."

"He would have brought me the moon."

"I know, you always said that."

"Oh really, well that's possible."

"You want me to tell you what I think? What makes me suffer? And explains why I'm crying? And what I understand all of a sudden, seeing Charlie's photo?"

"Yes, of course, Christine. Tell me."

"You expected to meet someone who wasn't nice. You

expected my father. But me, I would have preferred this young man there to my father." I hid my face in my napkin.

"No … Don't cry."

She had heard from him. Sixty years after they broke up he had tried to find her. He had been married, had had children, but he had never forgotten her. He had always thought that his life was more or less a failure, that he should have spent it with her. He had tracked her down. And had sent her a letter with his telephone number.

"It was weird. He has the voice of an old man."

"Go see him next time you come to Paris. Where does he live?"

"In the southern suburbs, I think. Near Essonne. Around there."

After lunch, we went for a walk. The next day we saw each other again at the same place. People were on the veranda or the terrace. It was still very hot. We sat at the same table as the day before. In the almost deserted room.

"I wanted to talk to you about something, Christine. You know, in one of your books, at one point, in *The Lover Market*, I think, Bruno says: 'Is that lady blind?'"

"Yes."

"At the moment, it gave me a shock, when I read that sentence. And then I thought about it. And I wanted to tell you." She paused, as if to swallow her saliva. "I wanted to say: yes. No doubt I was blind. Believe me when I say I regret it. I was so blind, so blind. So blind."

"Don't cry. Don't worry, Mama." There was a long silence. I looked at her face. "You are a fine person, Mama."

"What does that change?"

"That changes everything. Everything. We just have to admit that there are people who are not good people." A tear ran down her cheek. A little isolated tear. "You know, Mama, there are things I'm not proud of, me too. For how many years did I denigrate you?! Huh?! For how many years did I go along with my father's game? Do you think I'm proud of that? Starting from the moment I met him, I began to disparage you. You. To depreciate you. To criticize you. When I loved you so much. So much, Mama. It's no good. It's no good. I was no good. It's deplorable. Today I'm ashamed. I'm ashamed that I did that. That I demeaned you. During that whole period, and for so long. You think I don't regret it? You think I'm not angry with myself? I'm so ashamed."

"That was adolescence."

"Yes, oh, are you kidding? Do you really think it was that?"

"At the time, people said that a lot. There was a whole discourse about the angst of adolescence, all that stuff."

"Aside from my childhood, when I adored you, I have the feeling I have spent my life criticizing you. Forgive me, Mama."

"Probably I provoked that. Maybe I even sought it out. I was rejected so much. On that topic, actually – well, it's not directly connected but anyway. I wanted to tell you that I read your article about shame in *Libération*. And that text shook me up, a lot. I didn't talk to you about it right away. Because it disturbed me. It reminded me of times of great poverty that I lived through."

"What times?"

"Well, times I experienced. Things I felt a long time ago. But that mark a life, I believe."

"What moments did it make you think of?"

"Ohhh. Ancient things. Not very pleasant to think about them."

"Try to tell me."

"I can give you one or two examples, if you like, since it seems to interest you …"

"Yes, I'd like that."

"Okay, I'll tell you any which way, out of order … as it occurs to me …"

"Yes."

"Well, the shame of profound poverty, for example, for me, it's … I'm just mentioning it …"

"Yes yes."

"Being ashamed to go to school in the winter with summer sandals. Being embarrassed when people look at your feet. Being ashamed to be very shabbily dressed. Being ashamed to see the nun who came to give injections to my grandmother hand a five-franc bill to my mother, who had nothing to buy food with." She was looking at me while speaking. "Your accepting and understanding, because you were asked to, that Santa Claus hadn't been able to think of you at all. Seeing Mama go to the Gestapo's office just before their departure to settle a little bill for ironing that hadn't been paid. She who was so fearful, she came back with her money. I remember how proud she was for having dared to go there."

She looked out the picture window as if my grandmother was just going by.

"Would it bother you, Mama, if I make notes about what you are telling me?"

"No. It doesn't bother me. And there is something else I wanted to tell you, Christine."

"About shame?"

"Yes."

"What?"

"You always thought I didn't think much of the somewhat unpleasant environment of the ZUP and later Châtillons. You are mistaken. It was very difficult. At the same time, they represented a certain security. A little bit of affluence that showed its face little by little. I so wanted to give you a better life, the possibility of schooling, a different framework for life."

She was twisting her ring around her finger. A ring with seven interconnected sections that André had given her when they got married. And her gaze went from the picture window to my face.

"Today, you see, I have no end-of-the-month worries. And yet." A server came and asked us if we wanted any dessert. We said no. He left.

"And yet?"

"And yet. Yes. If I told you that I sometimes think of the ZUP with regret … Or of Châtillons … And even of the days when I was doing my accounts and you said to me, 'You sure do interesting things, Mama!'"

"I said that?"

"Yes, you said that. You were cute, you know. I had a cute little girl. And we were fine. I can't seem to tell you things exactly the way I'd like. It's hard sometimes to express certain feelings. I would so much love to be able to express what I feel. But intimate things are the hardest to express."

"That's true."

"I remember one year we lived in the ZUP that was particularly good. It was the year you turned ten. It was a really happy year. It was after May '68. There'd been a new feeling of freedom. You were happy. You were proud that your age had two digits. As for me, I had found a professional circle at Gireugne that suited me. You had your school, your girlfriends. Everything was good. It was a period of calm. We loved each other, we were good together, we laughed a lot. You used to say, 'You're cheerful, Mama.'"

"I know. I remember."

"It was a very good year, that one year. We went on vacation for the first time in a long time. To Kerpape."

"That's where I met a little girl named Christelle?"

"I don't remember her name. But you had met a little girl of your age, yes. A little Belgian girl. That was a very good vacation. There was nothing in particular. But there was sweetness." She had tears in her eyes. She wiped the corner of her eye then looked at the little tear on the tip of her finger. "Now I have a different life. Maybe I am a different person, even. But I've always kept in mind the memory of that year you turned ten. There was nothing extraordinary, though. And things were not any easier. Well, anyway! All those things, you see, were stirred up by your article on shame. They're little things. It's nothing. There! That was a little plunge into the past."

"We could write to each other when you return to Montpellier, Mama … What do you think?"

"That would be so good. I would like us to have regular exchanges like that. It would maybe seem less artificial than a quick telephone call. Well, that depends …"

In front of the restaurant there was a large square, or rather a large intersection crossed by two great boulevards and diagonal streets. A Citroen *traction avant* went by.

"Look, Mama."

"Oh yes, a Citroen *traction avant*." We watched it go by.

"I remember when I was little we would see them still."

"You know, sometimes when I think about the past, I ask myself where that whole world has gone. And if it really existed. I say to myself, 'Where is the world I used to know?'"

"We loved each other a lot, Mama."

"That's all we had!" She was silent. Then I said:

"Do you still have your moonstone necklace?"

"Moonstone? I had a moonstone necklace? No. I don't think so. You're wrong. I never had a moonstone necklace."

"Yes you did, come on. You know, it was a long necklace with blue-green stones, translucent, oval."

"Oh yes! I see what you're talking about. I had forgotten about it, you see. I also had a seahorse, with beautiful green eyes. That your father had given me. But I threw it out after his visit to Châteauroux when he announced he was married."

"May I ask you a completely unrelated question?"

"Of course."

"Did he talk about the Jews sometimes?"

"Yes. It wasn't very positive."

"What did he say?"

"Little things, in passing. It was never a long speech, just a word here, a phrase there."

"What, for example?"

"Little things. I tried not to pay attention."

"He knew you were Jewish?"

"Of course."

"Give me an example."

"Well … I dunno. You know, I …"

"A single one? You must remember something."

"He thought they were intelligent, but you had to pay attention, be wary of them. They were people who wanted to get things. You had to be cautious. It was words like that, he'd drop words. And he was against Israel. I remember one sentence, I still have it in my head: 'Taking over a country like that!'"

"Hmm."

"He would say that with a shocked tone. Like the tone of someone who didn't think it was right. 'Taking over a country like that!' I remember. I remember it well. 'Taking over a country like that!' That's what he would say."

"In front of you! Without taking any precautions?"

"It was never said directly about me. It was just said in passing."

"Were you hurt?"

"Yes, I was a little hurt. I didn't say anything. I didn't answer."

"Hmm. I understand."

"I didn't respond."

"You didn't go into it in depth …"

"No, I didn't go into it in depth. I didn't want to. I didn't want to discuss it further, I think. So I didn't make a point of it."

"I understand."

"If you make a point of it, you end up getting hurt more deeply."

"That's for sure. I understand. I think I understand what you're trying to say."

The next day we met again at the same spot. All week we saw each other at this café. At the same table. Inside, not far from the door. To be near the breeze. It was very hot. We stayed at least three hours each day. People were waiting in line for the veranda or the terrace, inside it was always just as empty.

"May I ask you a question?"

"Of course, Christine."

"How come you didn't see anything?"

"I can tell you that I'll regret it all my life."

"Retrospectively, do you understand why?"

"I had lost confidence in us."

"Which means?"

Her hands were flat on the table. Beautiful hands, fair skin, slender fingers, the joints maybe a little swollen by age, the nails filed in a rounded shape and discreetly polished.

"When you came home after seeing your father, you were in a bad way. And I used to think it was because you were back with me. I had lost confidence in our affection. I was blinded by that. I had lost confidence. In you. In us. In our affection. That blinded me. And I can tell you, Christine, right to the end of my life, I'll regret it. I would say to myself, it's normal, she's sick of her mother. I had a total loss of confidence. In us. In our relationship. In you. I would say to myself she's discovering something more rewarding. I didn't imagine that there could be another reason for your condition. I thought you were in a bad way because you didn't want to see me, to be back here with me. Because you didn't love me anymore."

"Really?"

"Yes."

"Really, that's what you thought?"

"Yes. Really. It was also a lack of confidence in myself. Of course. I had been rejected by my father, I had been rejected by your father. I thought it was normal for you to reject me. In comparison to your father, I was less educated, less intelligent, of a lower class socially. I thought you had made your choice. It seemed logical to me. For me, it was normal."

"Why didn't you say anything to me when Marc told you what was going on? Afterwards, too, when you came home from the hospital, you didn't say anything to me."

There were a few seconds of silence. A minute.

"I will never be healed, until I die, for not having said anything, not having done anything, not having seen anything. Such blindness! My God. Such blindness!"

"But you know, Mama, I think there is a logic to all this."

I had started to call her Mama again during the course of that week. And even using the word when it wasn't necessary. To have it in my mouth. And make it resonate in her ear like a little bell at last repaired.

"There's some logic, Mama, there's some logic to all that. There is an ironclad logic. It's not a little personal story, you understand, it's not a private story. No. This is not what you call private life. In this case it's the organization of society that's involved, through what happened to us. How people select others. It's not the story of an ordinary little woman, blinded and losing confidence, and it's not the story of an idiot either. It's a lot more than that. Because why does she lose confidence? You are right to say that you were rejected. It's a vast enterprise of rejection. Social, thought out, willed. Organized. And accepted. By everyone. This whole story, that's what it is. And right up to the end. Including what he did to me. It's something he did to you also, above all. It's the continuation of this rejection. To humiliate someone, the best thing to do is to make them ashamed, you know that. And, along with all the rest, just as you thought you had come out of the tunnel, what could make you feel more ashamed than that, than becoming the mother of a girl whose father did that to her? You were rejected because of your identity, Mama. Not because of the human being that you are. Not who you are, yourself. Not the person you were. And this rejection went so far as to do that to your daughter. It went that far. It went far. While still following the same logic. And the logic had to be pushed to its very limits. Since you had tried to oppose it. You were not to get out of your tunnel. All you could do was dream of getting out. Someone like you had to stay in the blind alley. Inside the tunnel, precisely, where you can't see anything."

"I don't really understand what you mean, Christine."

"Do you want me to tell you how I really see things? I am sure of what I'm saying. You might disagree. But I'm quite sure. The two of you belonged to different worlds, strangers to each other, at any rate that's how things were set from the start. And you accepted things being set that way. Because you were alone, because you were poor, because you were Jewish."

"Hmm."

"And with no one to protect you."

"That's for sure."

"And you were beautiful. Different from the others."

"Yes, well … ."

"Yes! It's important. That counts. Maybe you thought you were stronger. But he had warned you from the beginning, you could have contact with him, sure, but only him, his person, his private person. Contact with his social person – by which I mean his milieu, his identity – was out of the question. It was out of the question for your two identities to join together. They were not supposed to be in contact. He gave you compliments, naturally, but at the same time he took care to denigrate the social traces attached to you by culture and language. He gave you compliments but from on high, while observing your level and staying well above it."

"Oh that, he did consider himself very high above me. He considered himself above a lot of people, actually. He, his father, his family, you see, they weren't just anybody, he made sure I understood that."

"He also made sure you understood that he had a general understanding of society and that you didn't have that understanding. Since he belonged to a world superior to yours."

"On the social level, in any case, that was true."

"Yes, okay, and so ... And since his world was superior to yours, on several levels, according to their classifications, not only on the level of money, but also as they say on that of 'race,' let me remind you – one never speaks of it but for them it counts, it exists – there could not be social consequences between you. The goal was to make you lose. You could have a relationship, but on the condition that you respected certain rules, which guaranteed that you would not infiltrate his world. That there would be limits. The separation of your two worlds had to be established, and the superiority of his had to be maintained, well above. There couldn't be any fusion. Therefore, obviously, he wouldn't marry you. So that was the base. And he wouldn't introduce you to his friends and family. That's why you could go live in Paris, but in a little room. You weren't allowed to have lunch Boulevard Pereire or eat oysters with the family. Having a child was possible, on the condition that it didn't make any changes in the order and that he not recognize me. That's not a private story, you understand. That's not a personal arrangement, it's a social arrangement in which everyone participates, including you. It's the story of social rejection. And a story of selection. With the child, that made the exercise more perilous, therefore more interesting for him, more exciting. When there is a crisis and a value resists, that means the value is sure. Like Paris real estate after the 2008 crisis. You understand? It resisted. And well, they, likewise, resisted, even though there was a love story and a child you desired. That's powerful. They are powerful. You lead someone very close to the goal she'll never reach, and at the last moment you knock her out, KO. While saying to her, with your foot on her chest, that you had told her from the start she could not win. That it was she who wanted to compete. You remind her, at the last moment, that she is only a piece of shit. You two could have a child, sure, a man and a woman can have a child, and even love each other, in principle, no problem. But that didn't bring you closer to each other. He warned you, he wouldn't recognize me. Having a child with you was like a test of solidity, if you see what I mean. He was interested in it. I'm going to have a child with her, but instead of raising her up, I'm going to plunge her down. I can readily have a child with her because it will not be my child, socially. She thinks she's won the lottery, that this is going to make her change milieus and go up two or three rungs on the ladder, whereas it's going to make her go down. And it won't change anything for me, he thinks, I'll still be up above. Because I'm up above by right, by nature. Touching the limit allows one to verify it. That excites them. Having a child, in those conditions, allowed verifying to what extent you were from two separate categories. It wouldn't change anything. On the contrary, he would be confirmed in his superiority. He could very easily have a child by you and remain superior, far above you in his world. Like a world champion who welcomes competition for his title but knows that the match is rigged, that the challenger will be disqualified. Because he's no match, he can't compete. That allows him to humiliate the challenger in public and make them lose the desire to compete. Who's facing him? He has someone, you, who thinks there is nothing to lose. Whereas there is. You didn't know it, but you had a lot to lose. Confidence. The feeling of being worth something."

"Actually, as soon as I announced I was pregnant, he went on vacation. He didn't change his plans."

"That was part of the logic. Without any guilt. With the feeling he had made the rules perfectly clear to you."

"At the time, I found it normal. That is … I didn't want to ask myself the question. And his family was in agreement with him. His father didn't seem bothered by the situation. When I went to see him, I was just a detail. And his mother's reaction too. Someone alerted me: 'Look out,' she said to him, 'she's out to grab the heir to a family fortune.'"

"There you have it. That's it. And after I was born he continued on his way without deviating. You were to remain socially separate, and that separation prevailed over all the other considerations."

"No doubt."

"And he, always convinced he has been clear, honest, and frank with you."

"Oh yes, he never reproached himself for anything."

"People like that, they never reproach themselves for anything. He had in fact told you it was a dead-end street. You took it at your own risk, knowing it led nowhere. You could visit it, walk on it. But sooner or later you were going to have to retrace your steps."

"And that's what I did, actually."

"Well, yes, since he had announced it from the start, like a sign at the entrance."

"And all along during the time we were together, he made me observe all the signs that proved his superiority, and that when it came to me, I was less good. What's more, he had the frankness to admit to me – maybe I've already told you this – that if I had

had money, things would have been different, he had said 'if you had been rich, I might have thought about it.'"

"There you have it. And *you* found that normal. Therefore, you ended up accepting his rejection of you."

"It was not easy. It was hard, because I loved him."

"But why, Mama, why did you love him?"

"I loved him. Does one know why one loves someone? I can't tell you why. That's how it was. Starting from the moment he came into my life … I couldn't see him leaving it. He had changed my life. I couldn't imagine it anymore without him. But then I was forced to. And that's when I understood it couldn't happen any other way. It's almost … how can I say it … not normal, but … It was the ordinary course of things. And I allowed him to reject me. That was hard. But it was only sorrow. And that sorrow ended up disappearing. I had read a sentence in Proust, in *Time Regained*, I think, about the fact that sorrow is what disappears the most quickly, he says it better than I do, obviously. I'll look for it. I had copied it down, I put it in my wallet, have to check if it's still there."

"And where things got complicated was with the indication 'father unknown' on my birth certificate. Because that you couldn't stand. You were willing to accept that you were rejected, but you did not accept that I was too."

"I couldn't. I didn't see why. I thought that was unjust. Wrong."

"Maybe, but it was part of the program. If I bore his name, and if I was recognized, there was no separation anymore. Between your two milieus. Between the two of you. And he was on a mission to keep it watertight. And push you down. Because there's his whole milieu, right, that holds his hand and gives him a leg up. But you stuck to your guns. With the support of judicial provisions. You wanted that indication to disappear and for the civil registry of his family to record that he was my father. And that I therefore belonged, half of me, to his milieu."

"Yes, since that was the truth."

"Don't you know that such people have nothing to do with the truth? Absolutely nothing."

"You think?"

"Yes. Nothing at all. It's not their problem. The truth is what they decree. It's not what is."

"It's possible."

"You spent years of energy, it was a long time, you started over several times. And you thought it was worth it, since after the death of his father he ended up promising to recognize me."

"At the last minute, he backpedaled again. I had to take up all my arguments from the start and convince him again."

"Right. In the end, you convinced him. Okay. And you went together to the civil registry office at the Châteauroux town hall. My civil status changed. At last. It was done. And I am recognized as his daughter."

"You were his daughter in any case. You are his daughter."

"Right. Except that it was contrary to the logic of their side. Contrary to what they wanted. So what could he do? Well, he found something. He ignored the fundamental prohibition for parents to have sexual relations with their children. It was maybe a fundamental prohibition, but it didn't concern him. Not him. As if he wasn't my father and I was not his child. He was above that, above you, us, above social rules in a general sense. Including the fundamental social rule – so very very high above. Not to recognize a prohibition that applies to everyone is the supreme distinction. You understand! Such class! And for him, that was the ultimate way, the unbeatable way, to nullify the recognition. It goes way beyond the blood test. It's automatic negation. Change in point of view. The fundamental prohibition, now, is no longer the one about sexual relations between ascendants and descendants, it's the one about marrying below one's station. That way, there was still you on one side and he on the other. Because it was that, at all costs, that they had to preserve, for them that was the fundamental rule. He in his superior world, you in your inferior world. And on top of that, for you, in this inferior world, to make you even more inferior, to make you fall into the bottom of the bottom of the lowest of the bottom depths, as a premium, your daughter, raped by her father, and you the mother who sees nothing, the imbecile, the twat, the idiot, and – who knows – the accomplice even. You go down a few more rungs on the ladder of respectability, anyhow there is nothing lower. There is nothing lower than that. I'm sure of it, Mama."

"Maybe. But after all he was guilty of something very serious even so."

"Because you think a prohibition, even a fundamental one, was going to exclude him from his little society? When he's convinced of his superiority? And they are also. No. Therefore, he transgresses this prohibition to make you understand, *in extremis* – since you obstinately shove it into his face that I'm his daughter – that that's not how things go, not for them, he makes you go down another notch. You're the one who goes down. In their world one doesn't have a child with a Jewish woman, especially if she doesn't have money and there's nothing to get from her. Aside from her ass. Forgive me. I never talk like that, it's not my language, you know that. So he remains stable and reaffirms his rank, and you go down. In their logic, the points you made are not recognized. All those little judicial points. Your getting out of the tunnel, well, it won't get you anywhere. They're points that can be nullified, negated, each time you advanced a pawn on the chessboard, he found a way to make you retreat. And what he did with me is the last way he found, at the end of the road, to slam the door in your face and, to top it off, give an additional turn of the key in the lock. On the tactical level it's a masterful stroke. It's the stroke of a master. It's an apotheosis. And it's a definitive stroke. After that, there's nothing to do. Bring him to trial? That's not a real threat. There is nothing simpler than for a guy like him to deny it. To act like he's been slandered: attack on private life, on men, assumed holocaust deniers. Besides, you didn't do anything. You didn't file a complaint, you said nothing, you did nothing."

"I had that infection, and was hospitalized …"

"What kind of infection was it?"

"An infection of the fallopian tubes."

"As if by chance. The *tubes!* Your illusions had just gone down the tubes. Woah."

"Ah. That's how you see it?"

"Yes."

"In any case, I was in the hospital, and that weekend, as a result, you didn't go see your father in Paris, because I had just been hospitalized …"

"I know that, you've always told me that. But that doesn't take the place of speaking – getting an infection and going to the hospital. It would have been better if you had been able to say something to me."

"Probably I couldn't do anything different."

"It doesn't matter, Mama." I placed my hands on hers. We stayed like that for a long time. Not saying anything, one on each side of the table. Her hands were warm. "Are you okay? It's not too hard on you, this conversation, Mama? In any case, we got out of it somehow. And our life isn't over. You are beautiful, you know, Mama. You are still magnificent."

"That's sweet."

"No. It's true."

"You see me through your eyes …"

"I feel you are tense. Are you? Maybe it's all these topics you don't want to think about."

"It's not only that. It's that … You see … How can I say it. I would really have liked to keep intact the memory of the good times I had with him. We had some really good times. We spent some good times, you know, the two of us. We had marvelous times. Really. We had times … Really some beautiful times. A weekend in the Creuse region. A marvelous week at Beaulieu-sur-Mer. But with what went on afterwards with you, it wasn't possible to keep them like happy memories. I would have liked to. But there you have it. That's how it is. And starting from the moment when I couldn't keep the memory of the very good times we had, I preferred not to think about him at all, or about what we had together. We had some good times. Some very good times. There were beautiful things. I really would have liked to keep the memory of them. But it's not possible. I would have liked to keep inside me a few beautiful things, in my memory."

She picked up her purse from the floor, she searched inside, and she smiled. She was holding a little piece of paper.

"Look at this. Here's the sentence from Proust, it's here: 'Of the state of mind which, in that far-off year, had been tantamount to a long-drawn-out torture for me, nothing survived. For in this world of ours where everything withers, everything perishes, there is a thing that decays, that crumbles into dust even more completely, leaving behind still fewer traces of itself, than Beauty: namely Grief.' When I read that, I said to myself, *That's it.*"

"Do you remember when I met my father in Strasbourg?"

"No, not very well."

"Can't you picture the hotel? The hotel room where I saw him for the first time?"

"No."

"You can't picture any details? You don't remember that the walls were yellow?"

"No. Nothing."

She looked at me, embarrassed.

"You don't see any image?"

"None, no. I know we spent one night there. That there were two rooms on the same corridor. He came to see me in the evening."

"You were happy he came to see you?"

"Yes, but then he left. Not very late. He didn't stay the whole night. We had started having relations again. That evening in particular. But he went back home immediately afterwards."

"The moment I threw myself into his arms. You can't see that? The first time, in the room? You don't picture it?"

"No, for me there's a sort of curtain there. I can't picture anything."

"And the lunch just after, at the café in the train station, can you picture that?"

"Not that either. There's a veil over it."

"He had advised us to order *choucroute*. Do you remember? Nothing? How we were seated, nothing?"

"I don't remember."

"You can't remember anything?"

"I remember that the first time you talked to him on the phone, in Toul, it left a deep impression on you to hear his voice. You started to cry into the telephone. Because you were hearing his voice."

"At what moment?"

"It was quite quick. You spoke, then you heard his voice. And at that point you had a reaction. An emotion. Your tears came suddenly. You couldn't talk anymore. Then you recovered. The two of you didn't talk for long."

"I gave the phone back to you?"

"Yes."

"And what did you say to each other? Do you remember?"

"I must have discussed with him the fact that we were going to move to Reims ..."

"And the times before. Gérardmer, all that … Can you picture those times?"

"Yes. Better."

"I can't picture them. What was it like then?"

"You were little. You were what, four years old? You were so happy, you were happy to be with him, you called him Papa. There was also Lons-le-Saulnier. I remember you walking with us. There are a lot of things I can't picture. I remember us spending the day together, all three of us walking."

"You were happy?"

"Was I happy? I suppose. Like I was every time I saw him."

"After the meeting in Strasbourg, he came to see us at Gérardmer … The following weekend … Do you remember?"

"Of course."

"So there, how were things for you? Because that's where it started."

Her eyes hardened. She pinched her lips.

"That was the start. Not much, but it was there. At that time, how did it go for you? Tell me."

"I was happy, like I was every time I saw him. And I was sad when it was time to go. We were standing behind the car, you and I, we watched it leave. You understood that I was sad. And you made an affectionate gesture toward me."

"What did I do?"

"I don't remember. But you made an affectionate gesture."

"You don't remember what it was?"

"I think you touched my arm."

She returned to Montpellier a few days later. We began to talk on the telephone more often and more regularly.

"Hello."

"It's me, Mama. Am I disturbing you?"

"A bit. I have some guests."

"It's not important, nothing special. Have a good day, Mama. I give you a kiss."

The next day she sent me an email.

"I regretted not being able to talk to you yesterday, but it wasn't easy. The day was pleasant. Otherwise, no changes, the days continue to go by nearly the same.

"As I read your manuscript, I noticed a few little things to mention to you, at some point. Are you interested? It's up to you. Nothing very important.

"I often think about you. These days I've been remembering Rue de l'Indre, especially the lane, the garden, the huge chestnut tree. I've been remembering how I used to pick cherries. How I brought back armloads of lilacs. There was a kind of freedom that I didn't realize. But enough nostalgia, it's today and it's now."

archipelago books
is a not-for-profit literary press devoted to
promoting cross-cultural exchange through innovative
classic and contemporary international literature
www.archipelagobooks.org